D1241042

MEN IN THE FIELD

Cluny Classics

ROBERT HUGH BENSON
Come Rack, Come Rope
Dawn of All
The Light Invisible
No Other Gods

ORESTES BROWNSON
Like a Roaring Lion

G.K. CHESTERTON
A Chesterton Reader

GERTRUD VON LE FORT
The Veil of Veronica

NATHANIEL HAWTHORNE
The Shattered Fountain: Selected Tales

FRANÇOIS MAURIAC
The Dark Angels
The Desert of Love
A Kiss for the Leper
The Lamb
The Unknown Sea
Vipers' Tangle
What Was Lost

SIGRID UNDSET
The Burning Bush
The Wild Orchid
Images in a Mirror
Madame Dorthea

GEORGES BERNANOS
Joy
Under the Sun of Satan

MALACHY G. CARROLL
The Stranger

MYLES CONNOLLY
The Bump on Brannigan's Head
Dan England and the Noonday Devil
Mr. Blue
The Reason for Ann & Other Stories

ALICE CURTAYNE
House of Cards

CAROLINE GORDON
The Malefactors

ELISABETH LANGGÄSSER
The Quest

DOROTHY L. SAYERS
Whose Body?

IGNAZIO SILONE
Fontamara
Bread and Wine
The Seed Beneath the Snow

LEO L. WARD
Men in the Field: Eighteen Short Stories

MEN IN THE FIELD

EIGHTEEN SHORT STORIES

Leo L. Ward, C.S.C.

With a Foreword by JOHN T. FREDERICK

CLUNY
Providence, Rhode Island

Cluny Media edition, 2020

This Cluny edition is a republication
of the 1955 University of Notre Dame Press
edition of *Men in the Field: Eighteen Short Stories.*

For more information regarding this title
or any other Cluny Media publication,
please write to info@clunymedia.com, or to
Cluny Media, P.O. Box 1664, Providence, RI 02901

VISIT US ONLINE AT WWW.CLUNYMEDIA.COM

ISBN: 978-1950970759

Cover design by Clarke & Clarke
Cover image: Edvard Munch, *The Haymaker*,
1917, oil on canvas
Courtesy of Wikimedia Commons

CONTENTS

FOREWORD

There has been much talk about literature of midwestern farm life in the more than forty years since Willa Cather in *O Pioneers!* showed the world that there is the substance of great art in the lives of farmers in the region between the mountains; but not much of that literature has been written. There have been Miss Cather's own further studies, in *My Antonia*, *One of Ours*, and *Obscure Destinies*. There have been the novels and the profoundly satisfying short stories of Ruth Suckow—but most of these have treated the midwestern small town rather than the farms around it. There have been the fine poems of James Hearst; Josephine Johnson's tragic masterpiece, *Now in November*; other scattered examples of genuine insight and power. But most of us who have tried to write about midwestern farmers have not known their life well enough to grasp its essence, or have fallen short in perceptiveness and sympathy, or have not worked hard enough, or simply have lacked ability to meet the challenge of the task.

In *Men in the Field*, the days and ways of the real cornbelt farm of a generation ago are seen for the first time clear and whole. Leo L. Ward knew this life intimately and lovingly. No detail of fact or function escaped his attention; no variation of attitude or experience exceeded his understanding. The range of these unpretentious stories is amazing. There is the broad humor of "Balaam in Burrville," the living folklore of "Tobe Snow," the all but unbearable poignancy of "Winter Wheat," the stark tragedy of "Possession." Wholeness of vision marks this book, to a degree all but unique. Other writers have seen chiefly the misfits, the grotesques, the tortured and defeated workers on the land. Here the eccentric Burl Teeters is only one member of "The Threshing Ring;" and the tolerance of the others—the steady, the adequate, the successful men of the land—exasperated but amused, inexplicable to the city man, is but one example of the total comprehension which marks every story in this book.

The fields are here. Love of earth is of the innermost tissue of this fiction—a most keen and complete awareness of color and form, of scent and texture, of sky and air and soil: the "silvery green undersides" of burdock leaves and "black-purple" in the growing corn. The men are here, in all their pitiful and wonderful human variety, viewed with compassion and with respect, portrayed with tenderness and strength. These stories hold not merely the exact detail, the face and form of the corn-farm life, but its spirit. Their flawless reality is a means to an end: the illumination of universal human experience which is the unmistakable and ultimate mark of great art.

Leo L. Ward was the best of men, the best of friends, and in his place and time the best of writers.

John T. Frederick
Notre Dame, Indiana
May 1955

1.

THE THRESHING RING

Larry Martin, the station agent at Flora, stood with a hand shading his eyes in the door of the little dull green station. Scattered in little groups along the platform were the blue shirts and wide straw hats of many farmers. The men were gazing into the distance where they could see nothing except the glint and quiver of the two rails which joined and disappeared just before they reached the cleft in the bluish line of woods a half-mile away on the prairie.

"Forty-eight just left Shelby," the agent was saying in a loud, hearty voice meant for everybody on the platform. "Ought to be comin' any minute now. Phelps over at Shelby said she pulled out of there already." There was a short silence; then a murmur of eager talk swept along the station platform. "Yeah, yeah, there she is! Smoke up there in the woods now. And she's coalin' hard, looks like. I tell you, boys, haulin' threshing machines, takes coal for that." Larry Martin's loose blue shirt quivered as he chuckled and looked at three or four farmers standing near him on the platform. All the squinted faces in front of the station suddenly broke into pleased grins.

"About the first threshin' rig you ever unloaded, ain't it, Larry?" It was Jay Westwright who spoke in an even, controlled tone from where he stood beside the station agent. Westwright was a tall, straight man, with a strip of grayish hair showing beneath his wide hat on either side of his long, thin face.

"Yeah, first threshing rig we ever put down here. What is it? Red River, didn't you say?"

"Yeah, Red River Special. Farmer's Friend, they call it." Jay's long face turned to gaze proudly up the track again.

A short distance up the platform and out at the very curb, stood a little man with a slight bump high on his back. This was Burl Teeters, and he was gazing very fixedly and very thoughtfully up the track, his sweat-stained straw hat tilted far back on his little bald head and his hands shoved deeply into his belt. Beside him were the two Hamel boys, both also looking into the distance. Burl seemed to pay no attention to the excited talk going on all about him, except to throw an occasional scowl over his shoulder when Jay Westwright was talking. From time to time Lar and Zeb Hamel turned bearded faces to listen to what the station agent was saying.

"Where you goin' to set her down, Larry?" Jay Westwright asked. "Marley Simms over at the elevator said we could get all the water we wanted right there at the engine room. Wonder if we could set her down over there beside the engine room."

"Sure, Jay. We'll set that rig down about just anywhere you boys want."

"Think that would give us room, Mr. Kenyon? Right in there between the grain office and the engine room." It was in a quiet, respectful tone that Westwright asked the question of a youngish but serious looking man who stood beside him. The youngish man wore a pair of neat blue overalls, above the bib of which a white collar and a narrow dark tie showed. He was Mr. Kenyon, the expert who had arrived yesterday from the factory.

"Yes, that will be all right. That will give us plenty of room." Kenyon spoke in a firm, quiet voice, and with a thin, quick smile.

"It's a pretty big machine though, ain't it?" asked Larry Martin. Everybody turned again at the sound of the agent's loud voice—everybody except Burl Teeters, who had now moved a few steps farther up the platform.

"Yeah, it's a forty-five inch rig," Jay said. "Thirty, forty-five, of course. Had to be that big for a ring of our size."

"Well now, if that ain't enough room..."

"Oh yes, that will be plenty of room, boys—plenty." The youngish man in the neat blue overalls shook his head decisively.

Inside the station a thin insistent ringing suddenly drowned the monotonous chatter of the telegraph, and the agent, as he turned to the door with a wave of his black satin half-sleeve, shouted back to everyone on the platform. "Well, there she is, boys. She's comin' right in."

The wild, prolonged, shrill of a whistle came from up the tracks. Little clusters of men edged farther out on the platform, and there was a murmur of subdued talk. Piggy Bailey jumped down from his perch beside a striped canvas mail bag on the station truck, and pushed the truck out to the low curb of the platform, where he stood with one arm resting jauntily on the mail bag as the tall black bulk of the engine came rolling and grinding toward the station. The little clusters of men suddenly shrank back closer to the station as the engine came nearer.

Piggy Bailey was shouting at the engineer. "Got any thrashin' machines on this here train? We don't want nothin' smaller than thrashin' machines in this man's town." The engineer merely waved a big glove genially as the engine went hissing and grinding past the station.

The crowd, which had become quite silent, was now watching the box cars go swaying slowly past, one after another. At last a glint of shiny steel appeared above the red top of a box car. Then everybody suddenly saw the hood of a threshing blower, and a moment later the threshing machine loomed beside the station platform. As the cars moved slowly past, the threshing engine became sharp and black against the blue sky and the separator incredibly huge and shiny. The flat car came slowly to a stop, blocking the street that ran past the station. Then the men—all except Westwright, Kenyon, the station agent and Piggy Bailey—began pushing and pulling each other off the platform into the street. Soon a chorus of jumbled talk arose out around the flat car.

A trainman came running along the tracks. Larry Martin was shouting to him to set the threshing machine over beside the elevator. In just a little while a series of clankings came along the cars, and the whole train seemed to shudder once or twice. Then the great black engine and the red, shiny separator moved slowly away from the station on the long flat car.

It was only a short time, however, before the threshing machine came floating back on the side tracks with a brakeman riding in front of it. Then Burl Teeters went hopping across the two sets of tracks toward the engine room at the elevator where he began waving directions to the brakeman. With a shriek of brakes the long flat car came to a stop just beyond the low red engine room.

A moment later Burl was clambering over the edge of the car. Though his hat fell backwards on to the tracks, he seemed not to notice it. Now he was up on the car. Without his big hat he looked ridiculously small beside the tall wheels of the threshing machine. He edged his way around one of the great wheels. Suddenly he reached up, grasped the flange of the big steel belt wheel and tugged at it violently once or twice. The wheel turned slightly, and Burl stood back looking at it quizzically as though only half satisfied. Then Piggy Bailey whistled shrilly through his teeth from the station platform. The whistle came clear and high above the mumble of talk from the crowd now gathered about the flat car. "Hey, there," Piggy was shouting, "Hey, Burl, you the engineer? Thought you were goin' to be the blower man." Burl grinned, a bit sheepishly. The crowd laughed. Then Burl shouted back at Piggy, "No sir, I'm the engineer on this rig. I'm not no' blower man." He turned again to examine the engine. Then he climbed up to the high seat on the tool box. With one hand on the steering wheel, he pushed a lever with the other. Now someone shouted at him again. "What do you think of her, Burl? Hey, Burl, think she'll run all right?" It was Ambrose Mull, a huge man with faded green suspenders curving tight over his blue stomach, who stood half way across the tracks. Ambrose chuckled to himself and turned to grin at Jay Westwright back on the station platform. Burl seemed at first to pay no attention to the shouting, but finally he turned to yell, over his shoulder, "Yeah, guess maybe she'll run all right." Then he started climbing down from the engine, but stopped to open the fire box and peer inside. When at last he was on the ground he turned to Bert Helker, a tall man with slouched shoulders, and one of the Hamels, who was standing very near the car, and pointed a crooked outstretched thumb up at the engine. He was telling them that the only trouble might be the boiler. It didn't seem built back over the fire box quite far enough. "But I reckon it'll work good enough. Work all right if you get the right feller firin' it."

Soon there were many men working busily about the flat car. Kenyon, the expert, was over there now and he was explaining to the men how to brace some huge timbers against the car. But above all the other noises, the hammering and talking and laughing, came the shrill voice of Burl Teeters in almost constant questions and suggestions. He kept asking Kenyon particularly whether he thought the timbers were large enough for "an engine as big as that."

After a little while Jay Westwright and the station agent came slowly across the tracks from the platform, the agent carrying a piece of paper in his hand. Then Kenyon moved out from among the men, and the three stood talking together in the shade of a maple tree over beside the grain office, while the work went steadily on about the flat car.

But Burl also left the car and went over to the three men standing beside the grain office. He faced Westwright. "Well," he said, "how about some coal, Mr. Jay? Ain't you supposed to be gettin' the coal? A man can't fire no engine on hot air."

"The coal'll be here in plenty of time. Don't you be worryin' about the coal, Teeters."

"Yeah, you think you're runnin' the whole works. Well, I'll tell you one thing you're not runnin'. An' that's the engine. I'm the one that's running that engine." Burl's voice, as always when he grew excited or angry, had risen so shrill and high that it was almost like a frantic tinkle above the noises back around the flat car.

Jay Westwright's thin face became still narrower and very hard, then slowly broke into a faint grin, as he turned to continue talking to Kenyon. Burl wheeled about contemptuously and went back toward the other men.

The lifting and bracing and wedging of the great beams went steadily on, amidst the constant loud talk and the shouted laughter of the men. But it was almost two hours later before the threshing outfit, by means of several heavy ropes and pulleys, was finally got off the flat car.

It was now standing out in the street, directly in front of the grain office. Wisps of steam were playing about the clean new cylinders, and black smoke was tumbling up lazily from the wide funnel of the engine over the street and across the roof of the grain office. Kenyon, the expert, stood between the engine and the separator, with one foot resting on the big red separator tongue, while he talked briskly with Jay Westwright and Bert Helker. He was asking about Teeters, whether they were going to let him try to run the engine, and Jay was saying that Burl could probably learn to run it all right, if Mr. Kenyon would just keep a close watch on him for a while. It would be easier than trying to stop him from going on the engine, once he got it in his head this way. Bert Helker's wide hat rim flapped agreement with Jay. But already Burl was up on the high platform of the engine, bent forward examining the water gauge. By this time a large group of men had gathered on the sidewalk in front of the grain office, and on both sides of the street little clusters of women, and clerks in aprons, stood watching the threshing machine.

Suddenly the brass whistle on the engine spurted steam. There was a deafening blast. With Kenyon standing just behind him on the engine platform, Burl Teeters slowly pulled a lever and the big belt wheel began to race idly. A moment later the engine moved forward with a great clank. The separator lurched once or twice. And then the threshing machine was going up the street under a cone of dense black smoke. Burl Teeters kept turning the steering wheel, now one way, now the other. The low, wide wheels of the separator wandered slightly to the right, then back to the middle of the street again, and as the great machine moved on, the lugs of the engine wheels left a waving track behind them. From the door of the butcher shop Hunk Keller in his splotched white apron shouted to Burl above the puffing of the engine and the rumble of the separator. "Hold her down there, Burl. You better watch the speed limit." Farther up the street Joe Neff, standing on the curb in front of the pool room, lifted his shrill, whining voice to ask, "Where's your firin' cap, Burl? An' say, you ought to wear gloves for that. Where's your gloves, Burl?" Burl Teeters seemed hardly to hear the shouting, but only turned from time to time to say something to Kenyon, whose eyes never left the engine all the way up the street.

The threshing machine had soon passed from between the two rows of little wooden store buildings and had entered the lane of dense maple trees beyond. Through the trees the smoke floated upward, fading into the clear blue sky above Flora. At last it was becoming smaller and smaller out at the end of the street, and then on the road that led away from the town. But some of the men in front of the stores kept watching the threshing machine until it was only a black dot out in the level haze of the wheat-fields.

The threshing was beginning at Bert Helker's place, for Bert was at the north end of the ring and it was his turn this year. They had started in the afternoon when the grain would be quite dry, and by two o'clock they had already threshed off four loads of bundles.

Now two more wagons pulled in very close to the sides of the machine and the men began pitching the sheaves off their tall loads onto the conveyor, where the sheaves went leaping, one after another, into the dusty mouth of the separator, to be swallowed behind the flashing knives which fed the cylinder. In a little while three or four other loads came up, to await their turn back behind the engine. The drivers all climbed down from their wagons and gathered in the shade of one of the loads, where they watched the threshing with pleased grins on their faces.

Over beside the engine stood one of the Hamel boys, leaning on a pitchfork and talking to Burl Teeters, who sat, bent far forward, on the high box of the engine directly behind the big belt wheel. Burl was wearing a little black cap with a celluloid bill. With one hand resting lightly on tilted lever, he watched the separator closely, giving only occasional quick glances down at Hamel as he answered a question or asked the other man how he liked the "exack line on that belt there." Burl's eye followed the belt intently, where it dipped and twisted and came racing and flashing constantly back to the whirling drive wheel directly in front of him. Once he leaned far out and down toward Hamel, and with one hand pointing to the big belt wheel said, "See that belt there, Zeb—right in the same place on that wheel all the time. Tell you y' got to keep a good line on a belt for that." Then he quickly pulled himself up on his seat again, and the little black cap was craned far forward as before.

Up at the other end of the racing belt, the two men at the engine could see the big red separator only as a great blur of dust. Beyond that the flashing hood of the blower was belching forth its clotted stream of dust and straw in a slow semi-circle. But high above the nearer blur of dust, three men stood together on top of the tall separator. They were Kenyon, the expert, Jay Westwright, and Bert Helker. They were gazing into the dust below them, at the wheels and belts, and the sheaves that kept leaping into the mouths of the separator. From time to time, Kenyon and Westwright shouted to each other above the noise of the machine and Kenyon made frantic gestures, while Bert Helker listened curiously and nodded his straw hat until its wide brim would begin to flap. At last Kenyon leaned very close to the other two men and again shouted above the roaring whir beneath him. Westwright's and Helker's straw hats were tossed upward as if in laughter, and Kenyon lifted his hand to slap Jay on the back. But suddenly Kenyon reeled violently backward. He saved himself from falling from the top of the separator by frantically grasping Westwright's arm with his uplifted hand. Westwright himself staggered, and Helker had fallen in a clump where he stood. The separator had suddenly lurched under them, had literally jumped and then fallen back under them with a dull, loud clank.

There was wild shouting everywhere. But the three men on the separator did not hear it. They heard only the great clank of the machine beneath them, and then a sharp snap, followed by a clap as of thunder very near them, just in front of the separator itself. At the same instant Kenyon saw what seemed to be the broken end of a belt flying through the sky above him; while Jay Westwright saw two wagons turning rapidly in sharp circles away from the machine. Now the moan and whir of the machine suddenly ceased, and the men on the separator again heard the wild shouting of other men all about them. Then Kenyon, the expert, and Jay Westwright, the shrewd leader of his neighbors, and Bert Helker, who was curious and indolent above most men in this world, saw an extremely strange and monstrous thing. They saw the great black nose of the threshing engine coming straight toward them. Close below them now, directly in front of the separator, they heard the quick panting of the engine. The next moment Kenyon, the expert, was only a blur of arms and legs waving and tossing through the air—he had jumped from the top of the separator. The tall form of Bert Helker had shrunk into a ball on the high back of the separator. And now Jay Westwright was stepping backward in stiff jerks until he almost fell over Helker crouching behind him. Jay stopped rigidly, legs braced wide, one long arm stretched out desperately as if to defend himself, his narrow face lengthened into a stricken stare. Then he heard again the quick, sharp pant of the engine. He saw black tumbling smoke. For an instant he smelt hot grease and steam…

He remembered, an indefinite while later, having seen a sudden glint of something beside him, almost beneath him…like the shifting, shiny flash of a piston…and something huge and dark had passed by him. And nothing had hit the separator. There had been no terrific bump, no crashing of any kind…

Suddenly he knew he could see more clearly. He turned his head slowly, tautly sidewise. What he saw was strangely real and clear. It was the threshing engine moving rapidly away, circling out from the separator. As it moved away he saw somebody running after it. And he heard someone shouting wildly. He heard many men shouting.

The engine was stopped now. It was stopped out there beyond the low yellow slope of the straw stack. And Kenyon, the expert, was standing on the engine. One of Kenyon's hands was on a lever and his head was turned sharply toward the small humped figure of Burl Teeters on the platform beside him. But Burl's arms were folded lightly and the shiny bill of his little black cap was pushed carelessly up on his forehead as he stood there looking impertinently up into Kenyon's face. Neither of the two men was speaking at all, but simply staring at the other, until finally Kenyon turned abruptly to the levers and started the engine. He was soon bringing the engine around in a wide circle, and was half way back to the separator when Teeters burst into a wild shrieking almost in his ear. Above the loud rumble and pant of the engine there would occasionally rise a shrill word or two…"belt loose…tighten it…push too far…" Though Kenyon hardly seemed to hear all this, when at last he had brought the engine to a stop back hear the separator Burl was still yelling into his ear. He seemed to be saying something about a "lever slippin'." Kenyon, apparently not listening at all, looked critically down at the broken belt that lay twisted and sprawling along the ground. Several other men came slowly up. One after another they looked at the belt, then doubtfully up at Kenyon, then back at the belt again. Then every face suddenly turned again toward Burl Teeters, who was now leaning far out over the engine's tool box and shaking his short arm up at Jay Westwright, who still stood on top of the separator. Burl was all but screaming at Westwright, in a voice that sounded more than ever like the wild tinkling of a little bell. "Now you're satisfied, eh?" He kept repeating this almost in the same words.

Jay Westwright's head jerked backward. He looked at first startled, then bewildered. But slowly his long face shortened in a sneer, only to widen finally in a look of mingled contempt and pity.

Then with a quick leap Burl was on the ground. He came toward the separator in a half run and stopped just below the end of the conveyor. The yelling began again. "What you have to say about it? I'm just darin' you to say somethin'. I just dare you."

Finally Jay started to answer, and Burl stopped abruptly in a challenging silence. Jay's voice was strangely calm and steady. "No, I ain't got nothin' to say, Burl. I ain't sayin' anything to you. You just be quiet, an' let's not have any trouble. 'Nough trouble, as it is."

Burl stepped back from the separator a pace or two, then burst into a thin, piercing laugh. The laughter continued, growing higher and more shrill until at last it suddenly dropped to a sort of jerky cackle. Then Burl's face became smaller and menacing as he said, "Yeah, you won't say anything! You don't dare, that's what you don't. You don't dare say anything about my runnin' that engine. It's your fault anyway, an' you know it. You bought that engine an' you got slippin' levers, that's what you did. That's what caused all this." Burl's short crooked arm straightened a little as it swept the belt lying on the ground. "I ain't goin' to have nothin' to do with it. It's your fault anyways, 'taint mine. Buyin' that engine...it was all your doin's. Now just fix her up if you want to. That's what you can do."

Burl Teeters turned from the separator and started walking away in the direction of Bert Helker's barn up beyond the pasture. The slight bow in his legs seemed very wide as he went on with a kind of short stamping stride. Halfway to the barn he wheeled about and suddenly yelled back wildly at Jay Westwright, "If I hear of you sayin' anything..." His voice rose so shrill it became unintelligible. He turned again and went on toward the barn. And a little while later the men standing about the threshing machine saw Burl leave Bert Helker's farmyard in a buggy amidst a cloud of dust that kept following the buggy until it was beyond the hedge at the other side of the orchard.

That evening Jay Westwright, Kenyon, Ambrose Mull and three or four other men who had come over to Bert's after their chores sat smoking and talking around the feedway door of Bert's barn. Kenyon and Westwright were seated in the doorway. Bert Helker sat on a milk stool in front of them, and the others were squatting about on the ground amidst a litter of corn cobs that had been thrown out from the feed boxes. Occasionally a glow would come to the end of Kenyon's cigar, and then the glow would drop to his knee. The lights from three or four pipes kept brightening now and again.

"So you don't think it'd do any good to splice it, Mr. Kenyon?" Bert Helker asked.

"No, wouldn't do a bit of good." There was a prolonged glow at the end of Kenyon's cigar. "Splicin' couldn't fix it. That belt was ripped, if you noticed. All along one side.

And splicin' wouldn't do a ripped belt any good. Can't. Fabric's gone. Splicin' can't fix fabric like that."

"Looks like they ain't no way out of it. We'll just have to lay off a day." Jay Westwright spoke in a tone of reasoned finality.

"Yes. It'll take a day anyway to get a new belt in here. Even with telegraphing for it right off like I did there this afternoon."

"Funny, but I don't think I see yet just how he did it exactly, Mr. Kenyon." Bert Helker's head lolled slightly to one side as he looked at Kenyon and asked the question.

"Well, as I was tellin' you boys there this afternoon just after he stamped off like that..." Ambrose Mull, whose fat shoulders leaned back against the barn started to laugh, and the others followed him. Even after the other men had stopped, Ambrose still chuckled gutturally to himself over beside the door. "As I was saying this afternoon, Teeters must have been monkeyin' with the levers. It's the only thing could have caused it. Of course you heard him tryin' to make out the lever slipped." Kenyon broke into a short, dry laugh, but none of the other men laughed now. They were all listening intently and silently, all except Ambrose Mull who was still chuckling. "Why, a lever couldn't slip like that. No sir, not on a Red River engine it couldn't." "Yeah, I kind of think I see now," Bert Helker said slowly. "He just kind of pulled a lever, and then maybe pushed it too much. Got excited like when the belt broke. And as cons'quence ..."

"Exactly. He was just itchin' around the levers there. Couldn't keep his hands off them. Pulled one ju-u-ust a little, you know. Course the engine started to backin', nacherly. Then the belt snapped, you see. And then—then he got good and scared, and pushed the lever. Probably pushed it clear over. And then...well, the next thing we knew that engine was comin' straight for the separator. And boys, how it ever missed that separator is more than I know. Some things are just queer, that's all—I've always said that. Simply no way of explainin' them. And it sure seems like that was one of them, right there this afternoon ..."

Kenyon was silent for a while shaking his head solemnly while he looked down at the ground between his knees. Bert Helker on his milk stool pulled at his chin with a big hand. Ambrose Mull did not chuckle now, but only breathed laboriously over beside the door.

At last Kenyon's cigar glowed again, and he said, "Boys, I tell you if that engine had hit that separator..." He paused. "Well, it wouldn't just mean gettin' a new belt. Why, if you used it for kindlin' there wouldn't be enough of that separator left to start a fire in the morning."

In the stillness that followed, the dusk seemed to become instantly darker. In the west, very low and far away, only a faint blush was left along the sky. The men sat for a while in silence, watching this patch of light.

At last Kenyon stirred as if to get up from where he was sitting in the doorway, then with one hand grasping the jamb of the door he said in a matter of fact tone, "Well, I reckon we've lost an engineer anyway."

"No sir," Bert Helker had spoken up impulsively. "He'll be right back here, Mr. Kenyon. You wait and see if he ain't."

Ambrose Mull started sputtering and wheezing over beside the door. "Why, I'll bet ya he'll be right back here in the mornin' again, first thing. Sure as daylight he will. I tell ya, you don't know them Teeterses, Mr. Kenyon. Ya can't, unless you live right over there beside 'em like I do. Oh, I knows 'em, ever' last one of 'em. Knowed their dad afore 'em. An' they're all just the same. The whole lot of 'em always tryin' things they ain't got no business at. Messin' things all up ever' time. But you can't tell 'em nothin'. Can't never tell a Teeters nothin'. They're all half crazy, that's what they are. An' Burl, he's just about the worst of the whole keeboodle."

Another deep voice sounded, detached, as though the speaker was talking to himself, as it came out of the dusk before the barn. "Yeah, Teeters'll be back around that engine again. I just knows he will."

After a moment Kenyon spoke up again, speaking in a helpless, complaining tone. "But boys, what we goin' to do? Can't have that fellow back on that engine again." "Yes, but you'll never keep him off, Mr. Kenyon," said Jay Westwright. "He'll cause no end of rumpus to all the rest of the ring if we try it."

"Why, there ought to be some way of gettin' rid of him. We've just got to keep him away from that machine, boys."

"Can't never do it, Mr. Kenyon," Jay Westwright said, and Bert Helker repeated it.

"You never can," Bert said. "No use talkin'. You can't keep him away nohow. He's bound to be back."

"But couldn't you just kind of ease him out some way? Maybe get him out of the ring some way. Might buy up his share in the machine, boys. Couldn't you do that?" "Oh, I don't know, Mr. Kenyon," said Jay. "I don't hardly think we'd ought to push him out of the ring that way. Don't see how we could do it very easy even if we wanted to. He wouldn't sell his share to none of us. Wouldn't sell it now anyways."

"No," Bert Helker said, "I don't see how we could do that, Mr. Kenyon. Don't think the boys'd want to put him out exactly."

Then Jay's voice came in slow, measured tones. "Fact, there's only one way I see of doin' it. I know it'll be mighty awkward, but the only way I see is for you to stay right around that engine. Just practically run it yourself, Mr. Kenyon. It's the only thing I see we can do."

"Well, you boys ought to know best, of course," said Kenyon. "It will make it kind of bad. I'd ought to be up around the separator most of the time. But if that's the way you boys look at it I suppose it's the only way. You know, I want to be accommodating. That's what I'm here for. I want you boys to be satisfied."

"That's about the only way we can do it, Mr. Kenyon—the way Jay said," said Bert Helker. "Fer he'll be right back here, wantin' to run that engine again, sure as shootin'. You can't stop Burl Teeters, onct he gets somethin' like that in his head. An' he won't forget it either, like you might think after this afternoon. No way under blue heaven, a gettin' it out a his head. He's a Teeters, that's all, just as Ambrose says."

There was absolute silence for a while. Then away on the prairie, from the direction of the patch of light at the edge of the sky, there arose a thin, distant calling. The voice seemed very far away, yet it came very clear through the damp dusk.

Ambrose Mull grunted. "There he is now. That's him. I hearn him lots a times like that. It's just like him. That's a Teeters for you, callin' his hogs this time a night when ever' body else has his chorin' done and forgot about it a couple hours ago." Ambrose snorted and grunted a few times, and then was silent. Kenyon suddenly laughed, very briefly and as though to himself.

The thin distant calling continued, and now it seemed to be growing constantly clearer and stronger as it came out of the dusk.

The men sat for a while, silently listening. Moment after moment the calling grew still clearer and louder. But it was shrill and thin, somehow like an impudent, insistent challenge too distant to be answered at all.

Suddenly Jay Westwright rose impatiently to his feet. The others were getting up now, one after another, Ambrose Mull puffing and wheezing as he did so. Ambrose's puffing was the only sound made by any of the men, except a scuffling of feet and a light rattle of corn cobs here and there on the ground. The faint distant calling came again, more distinct than before. Then Jay Westwright's voice, lifted slightly as if with irritation, seemed to be saying something about a belt. Kenyon made some vague answer about "losing only a day or two." Other voices out in front of the barn were moving away slowly. But above the mutter and mumble of voices the thin calling continued to come, shrill and clear.

In a little while two or three buggies and one Ford were leaving Bert Helker's farmyard. The rattle of wheels and the quick fluttering purr of a small motor soon died away. Then the calling could be heard again, and it seemed even more distinct than it had yet been, a thin distant ringing that pierced the darkness which was settling everywhere over the prairie.

2.

DROUGHT

His pulse came like spurts of fever at his temples. It wasn't six o'clock yet, but the sun was already a white sheet of flame high above the prairie. The earth was like powder. He could feel its heat through his shoes as he walked on behind the horses. He pulled the team into the cornfield. As he worked about the plow, lifting the neck yoke and fastening the tugs, he heard the dry rattle of the corn blades whenever he brushed against them. He picked up the hues and stood for a moment looking across the fields out of closely puckered eyes. The corn stretched away, grayish and dead in the blinding light. He knew every blade in the fields was cooked and shrivelled by the drought. Farther away he saw other cornfields, mere strips of gray haze drifting toward the shimmering horizon.

The man stepped over the iron seat of the plow, then called to the horses in a hollow command. The team moved away into the field. A cloud of dust arose about the plow, almost hiding the man riding along on the low seat. The cloud, lengthening as the team walked on, kept crawling slowly across the field.

Sometimes at the ends of the field the man would let the team rest for a while before moving into the next row. The dust cloud would thin slowly away. The man would sit staring quietly at the horses. He could feel the dust stinging in his nostrils and choking him, the veins at his temples swelling and ebbing with his breath. He noticed the dirty splashes of white on the hind legs of the horses, where the tugs had rubbed the sweat to lather. He saw the quick movement of the horses' bellies as they stood there panting. Then his eyes would drift off over the field. Everywhere the heat was wreathing visibly upward from the earth into the vast white sky. Farther away he could see other teams plowing, dirty smudges of cloud trailing through a sea of quivering light.

The plowing continued. Row followed row, until the man's eyes were half blinded by the dust that kept puffing and eddying up from the ashy corn blades moving always beneath him. His arms ached and throbbed as they guided the heavy shanks. The sun burned through his clothes and crawled over his skin beneath his shirt and overalls. Sometimes his whole body felt parched and numb, as if all his blood were dry within him.

From time to time he took a drink of the warm water from the jug which he kept under the leaves of a burdock at the end of the field. He did not realize how hot the water was. It tasted almost fresh and cool to his parched lips. He would pour a little of the water over his dirty wrists, and maybe splash some across his forehead. Then he would put his wide straw hat back on his head, step on to the plow, and move into the field again.

Noon came. Amidst the intense stillness the tug chains clinked with a thin hot sound as he unhitched the sweating horses. Their stench was acrid as he walked through the dust behind them, moving slowly toward the barn.

The barn was full of dead, motionless heat. He quickly fed the horses, dumping the hard ears into their boxes, piling a large bundle of hay into the manger. He heard a slobbering and steady grinding as the horses bit into the corn. He tossed the pitchfork carelessly into a corner and went toward the house.

At dinner he ate mechanically, hardly saying anything, with his eyes fixed on the plate of steaming food. From time to time he could feel sweat coming on his brow and under his clothes. He heard his wife moving to and from the kitchen. Then he felt rather than saw her sitting there on the other side of the table. She seemed very far away from him, and strangely cool and comfortable. Even the child did not come to stand beside him now, or pull at his shirt and ask him to put jelly on her bread.

After another cup of the strong coffee he got up from the table and went out to the big maple tree beside the porch, where he lay wearily upon the shaded grass. The seared blades of the grass tickled the sensitive, burned skin on the back of his neck. A locust slit the noon stillness from high in the tree. After a while he seemed to awake suddenly from a kind of dull sleep. He got up slowly and moved away toward the barn. A quick chirping voice came after him. He turned and saw that it was the child standing with her mother in the door. The woman was smiling down at the child. He thought the thin voice was telling him to be sure and come back in time for supper. He managed to wave stiffly towards the house before stepping into the barn.

Out in the field the corn stood very still and dead about him. The iron plow was like fire when he touched it. As he rode off into the first row the sun began cooking his bent back. The sweat that had moistened his whole body during the noon hour was now dried into his skin. His clothes felt stiff and hard, like a sheath of hot metal enclosing his body. The heat wavered up from the dusty earth beneath him, parching the skin of his face to the crispness of paper.

Whenever he stopped at the ends of the field now, he saw the drooping heads of the horses through the lifting dust. Their sides still panted, but there were no patches of dirty lather on their legs. He knew that it had become so hot that the sweat was drying into their hides. Out beyond the team the prairie was more indistinct than before, a vague disk of seething heat.

Sometimes as he rode along above the rows he felt dazed for long moments and a quick lightness seemed to go eddying through his head. But this would go away again, and the dust and the heat would burn fiercely and steadily into his body as before.

After a while he tried to glance upward occasionally, as if measuring the slow decline of the sun. But the white flames burned down into his face, and only left a jabbing ache behind his eyes. After that the shanks would sometimes tear the cornstalks from the hills. But the man was too dazed to grow angry. He could only pull the shanks heavily back into place, and ride on in a kind of fevered stupor, feeling a strange indifference to everything.

Now an intenser stillness seemed to fill the whole prairie. Even the dust appeared to stand still about the plow. Only the heat moved, wavering steadily upward from the earth. But the man on the plow only felt the dead ache that seemed to go pounding through his body, and the dry flame that was parching his blood. He did not notice the intenser stillness that had come into the heat about him. He saw nothing of the cloud that had appeared at the western edge of the prairie.

At first it was only a dark spot beyond the white haze of horizon. But it spread rapidly upward and grew steadily darker. Soon it had become a mass of slaty blackness. And now it was shooting up from the earth in a column of solid murk, thrusting stark, jagged edges up the sky, yet moving always with a strange stillness and an awful strength, like some giant living thing.

Then far away, on all the low hills of the prairie, small whirling clouds of dust were rising. In one quick instant the wind had come rushing out of the black center of the storm.

The man on the plow had just turned the horses at the farther end of the field, to let them rest for a little while. He had noticed nothing of the rising cloud, but had gone on riding through the last corn row, half blinded by the dust. But before all the dust had risen from about the plow, a breath of the coming wind reached him. At first it came in quick hot puffs, then became almost immediately cooler and steadier. The dull eyes of the man opened in a wide, dazed stare over the heads of the horses. His mouth began working helplessly, like that of an excited child. His whole face was suddenly wild with gladness and wonder.

Just then the black cloud seemed to leap higher, seething and tumbling at its summit. Great piling billows spurted out from it, and broke in a mad race up the sky. The man still sat motionless upon the plow. His excited eyes watched the dark wall now reaching fiercely toward the sun. A few moments later he felt the shadow which fled swiftly over the field, past himself and his team. He knew the terrible white sky had been instantly blotted away. He saw the deeper darkness that now came quickly out of the west. He felt a new strength in the wind, pressing a fresher coolness into the burnt skin of his face.

The man was now climbing off the plow, as if only half realizing what he was doing. He stood there beside one of the high wheels, his tall figure leaning slightly forward into the force of the wind, his hat clutched tremblingly before him. His eyes were still fixed upward, staring with frenzied joy at the black, moving sky. But suddenly he seemed to see all the darkness rent into huge segments. Great prongs of flame shot downward across the sky. The man started hesitantly toward the team, as if vaguely remembering the danger of the iron plow. A moment later he ran to the horses' tugs and began unhitching with frantic haste. His voice now rose, shouting at the horses above the steady drone of the wind. Then just as the team moved slowly from the plow, the man felt the first great slashes of the rain drive past him.

At first the horses went reluctantly into the storm. But as the shouting behind them rose higher and higher, they soon broke into a lunging gallop along one of the corn rows. The man had thrown the buckled ends of the lines about his shoulders. And now he felt the horses pulling him violently forward. Each of his steps became a long easy leap into the full force of the storm. He could hear the vibrant roar of the wind in his ears. He felt the great sudden weight of the rain beating and crashing against him. Solid torrents of water poured over him, drenching his whole body. A great coolness kept flushing over his hot tingling breast. He felt the cold streams of the rain washing down his sides and his thighs. Sometimes his half closed eyes could see the dense banks of water that came dipping and plunging toward him just before they broke and went crashing past. And through every rift in the rain he saw his corn flashing and flashing beneath him. Suddenly he realized how all the fields of the prairie were drinking in the great coolness of the rain. A kind of crazed gladness seemed to possess him. His voice broke above the hollow roar of the wind. And now he was laughing, and shouting wildly, his voice sometimes rising almost to a kind of sobbing frenzy, as he went leaping on through the storm.

A half minute later the team swerved out of the cornfield in a dead run. They galloped on through the open gate of the farmlot and then came almost to an abrupt stop, slipping and splashing through the muddy puddles in front of the barn. The man flung the lines from his shoulders and ran to unsnap the team's checks. He slapped each horse over the rump as it scurried toward the barn. Inside the barn, there was a slight lingering heat. But the man only stopped to slip wet bridles from the horses' steaming heads. Then he stepped out of the barn and went toward the house in a kind of leaping run. Again he felt the storm beating over him, more violently than before. The rain swept between the house and barn in hard plunging gusts. He felt its cold spray stinging his face for an instant before each solid pile of water smashed against his shoulders. But the man leaned far forward as he ran, and he was laughing breathlessly as he leaped on through the storm. Then suddenly his house loomed before him out of a flying bank of rain.

The man lunged up into the porch, where he found his wife and his child waiting for him, huddled together back in the farthest sheltered corner. The woman was hugging the child deep into the knees of her dress. They both stared up at him, half fearful, half smiling. Suddenly the man broke into a chuckling laugh, then reached quickly down and yanked the child out of the woman's arms. He lifted her to his shoulder with a great swoop, then turned and pointed a wet arm out into the storm. The child's voice rose in a little whimpering laugh. The man's big hand pulled her head down into his bare neck, rumpling her curls over his wet face. But now he felt the woman frantically dragging the child down from his shoulder. He only laughed again, and went on gazing into the storm. He stepped out nearer the porch railing. The fine spray of the rain blew down from the porch eaves into his face. The man could feel little cold streams trickling down his neck, beneath his open shirt. He heard the constant tear and slash of the rain through the trees above the house. He saw, everywhere, huge masses of water looping and tumbling upon the wind. Between the driving gusts of the storm, he caught dim glimpses of his barn standing in a shiny black lake that covered the farmyard. Sometimes his eyes tried to peer past the barn towards his cornfields, but he could see nothing. Then behind him, as if far away, he heard the sudden voice of his wife. She was telling him, almost petulantly, that he should change his clothes—he was all soaked through. But he only laughed again, carelessly as if to himself, and went on gazing into the storm.

After a little while the man saw the solid walls of rain thinning and breaking in the wind. He knew the storm was slackening. Soon only heavy gusts of mist were blowing between the house and the barn. The wind now came in quick breathless puffs. It rose in a last wild gust, blowing all the mist before it. Then it seemed to die away, with a sigh that dropped down suddenly out of the wet trees. The dark heavy air was no longer streaked with rain. The wet barn stood black and sharp against a slaty distance. The corn beyond the barn lay dark and green like a lake rising out of the last mists of the rain.

The odor of damp earth came into the porch—the smell of wet grass, the fainter smell of wet corn carried out of the fields by the spent storm. The man smiled as his eyes moved slowly over all the stark outlines of the prairie. He felt the whole earth living again. And deep within him, he felt his breath coming fresh and cool.

He was turning from the porch rail, but stopped to look again at the prairie. Then cold dead air pushed suddenly up into the porch. The man felt its pressure against his cheek. His forehead was instantly white, and a quick fear had fixed the lines of his face. Now a kind of distant clattering arose. The man heard it growing louder, and coming rapidly closer. Then, only a few moments later, he saw the first white pebbles of the hail come dancing over the grass of the yard.

The man stood motionless upon the porch, his face stricken into a twisted stare. But his eyes saw nothing except the white slanting walls of the hail. He was only half conscious of the hollow din on the roof above him. He hardly heard the loud crashing in the trees above the house. He was listening only to a fainter shatter that came from farther away. The man knew this was the hail sweeping over all his corn.

Then the loud crashing had suddenly ceased. The man stared at the last tattered sheet of the hail moving past the black lines of his barn. He heard a thin clatter die away over the distant prairie. Then he felt only the great stillness that seemed to be settling everywhere over the earth.

Slowly the man's hands dropped and rested upon the railing before him. His shoulders drooped limply forward. His whole body was bent and humped over the railing of the porch. His tortured eyes were staring out at the cornfield beyond the barn.

But a wild glow was suddenly spreading everywhere before him. He saw it falling like red flame across his com. The sun had broken from the low west. Each hill of the corn now seemed to stand sharp and vivid before his eyes. But he could tell that the blades were all gone. He knew that he was looking only at the shattered and blasted stumps of his corn.

Suddenly he felt a hand pulling at his wet sleeve. He knew it was his wife. He heard her telling him that he should go into the house now. He kept his face averted while he spoke, for his eyes had become suddenly wet and blurred. "No," he said kindly, "I must go out to the barn now. Haven't even unharnessed the horses yet." Then he stepped heavily down from the porch and walked slowly away through the mud of the farmyard.

3.

TOBE SNOW

Tobe Snow went back to the time before the railroad, but you never could think of Tobe as coming to Prairie Green. You could only think of Tobe as being there from the beginning and the town growing up around him. Prairie Green had always needed Tobe Snow. He was marshal now—had been the town marshal for the last fifteen years. Before that he had been barkeep, and then harness maker.

Tobe was the kind of man who had never searched out opportunities. He didn't need to. His chances always came, soon or late. And in nothing more truly than talking. Tobe always had his say, and it was always the last say. He knew he was the best talker in Prairie Green. And though Prairie Green sometimes wagged its head and grinned, it also knew it. No man had ever grinned directly into Tobe Snow's face.

Usually he went around silent and tight-lipped, looking at Prairie Green, waiting till it was entirely ready to listen. He seldom wasted himself on small audiences. Some of the farmers tried to draw him out when they met him on the street on rainy days. But he would look at most of them as if they were utter strangers, with almost the same look that he gave to tramps and suspicious characters. Even Josh Bowdin, the big cattleman, never got more than a few words from him. And there was the time Josh asked him how long he thought the dry weather would last—Josh just stopping on the street and pushing back his wide hat, and asking the question in his big neighborly way. Tobe had said he wasn't even interested in dry weather. Said he was only thinking about when the rain would come. Everybody heard about it and used it on Josh for years, especially the farmers whenever Josh went out to buy their cattle.

But Tobe would talk when his words ran no danger of being wasted, when Prairie Green became entirely silent and respectful. This happened a few times a year, of winter evenings usually. Back behind the big round stove in Allison's Hardware Store. Tobe never talked much to Herb Allison personally. He just nodded whenever he went past the store.

But on bad winter evenings Tobe would come into the store mysteriously. He'd shake the snow off just inside the door, like a ghost suddenly stepping out of his sheets. Then he would come back through the store, saying nothing, and sit down. He always took the chair in the corner, unless Joker Harvey was there before him. Joker Harvey was a good talker too. He was the local butcher, and a physical giant, with a face that was merely a mouth in a great round clot of reddened beard.

Tobe Snow sat low in his chair, as if only half listening to the other men about the stove. His faded colorless overcoat was fastened up under his chin by a tremendous horse-blanket safety pin. Almost the only things you noticed about Tobe were his eyes, and his ears, which protruded, large and long, from under the shapeless hat that was jammed low onto his head. The small black pipe sticking out of his thin gray beard was insignificant, and Tobe never seemed to pay any attention to it. His eyes were only two watery beads. He hardly seemed to need them. Somehow you felt that he saw everything without looking at it, just as he heard the men talking around him without listening.

Perry Lawson, who owned the new elevator, was talking about the prices of grain. Tobe was apparently paying no attention, as if he knew that Lawson was mistaken. Somebody asked Lawson if he ever found out for sure about how the fire in the old elevator started. The men went on talking about the fire, speaking of how the grain kept burning for over a week. Tobe's eyes now became fastened on the coal bucket. Whenever anyone spat at the bucket and hit it squarely, his eyes widened as if in half conscious surprise. A grin was coming, stronger and stronger, on his face.

Suddenly his gray face lifted, and he looked up over the stove toward the front of the store, his eyes shining against the darkness of the corner behind him. The men stopped talking. Tobe waited till everything was quite silent. The faces of all the men turned toward him. He was still looking toward the front of the store as if waiting for a signal. At last his mouth pushed out in a slow, satisfied pucker, and he began.

I

"You fellers don't remember it," he said very slowly and evenly, in a high cracked voice. "It was away before your time. But there was a fire here at Prairie Green once that 'ud make your elevator look like a match aburnin' in the broad daylight."

The men glanced at each other across the stove. They had heard Tobe tell this story a few times before—on winter evenings like this, when he had risen to one of his rare great moments of talk. But no one smiled openly. They all looked back at Tobe with a show of eagerness. Joker Harvey even sat up in his chair with a long heaving effort of his huge body. Tobe looked around the circle and held the stub of his pipe before him with rhetorical suspense.

"It was the year after the railroad went through," he said as steadily as before. "I was barkeep in Nick Dodge's saloon. Nick was the best man ever came to Prairie Green. Me and him licked a dozen whippersnappers once. Licked 'em to a frazzle. They came into the saloon, agoin' to paint things up. Nick never'd stand for that. So me and him just laid 'em on the floor, one after another. Then I watched the place while Nick whipped 'em clean out a town. Whipped 'em right out a town with a black snake. That's the kind of feller Nick Dodge was."

Tobe looked down at the coal bucket for a few moments, in eloquent modesty, or in memorial respect for the name of Nick Dodge. Then he went on. "Well, I was barkeep for Nick, and it was the year after the railroad went through. Dryest year I ever seed. Never did rain that summer. Everything was just like paper. Then one day didn't there a fire start on the railroad. Out on the prairie. And a hot wind blowin' too, right out of the southwest. That fire just spread out and kept a spreadin'. Of course it came straight for town. You could see it out there, comin' too fast even to make hardly any smoke. Only just red devils of flames leapin' and jumpin' everywhere, and comin' faster 'n a pack of wild horses. You didn't have time to do nothin'. Up to the ring of safety furrows at the edge of town before you knew it. And it came right over them safety furrows. Caught in some trees a dude feller had around his house out there. A feller that was here on the railroad. A kind of manager feller that was runnin' the railroad when it first come. Little trees he had planted around his house out at the edge of town. Even the trees was all dried up that summer. And then there wasn't any stoppin' it. Came right up through the town. Catchin' on roofs. Houses goin' up faster than brush piles. Only it seemin' to leap clear over some a the houses that were kind a off to themselves. And that fire, comin' like it did, course it wasn't goin' to spread back and catch 'em when it missed 'em once. Few of the houses saved that way. But the people, they was runnin' every which way, tryin' to keep out a the fire. Just plumb crazy, all of 'em. I seed somethin' had to be done right off. Nobody doin' nothin' but runnin' for his hide. Course I was thinkin' specially of women and children. I seed the fire was gettin' right into the business places along the street here by that time. So I had to think mighty fast. And all at once I hit on an idea. Nick Dodge had a lot of beer down at the station. Just shipped in. Not even unloaded yet. About twenty or thirty barrel anyway. Or maybe more'n that. Maybe fifty barrel. Anyways, I went out and got hold of Nick. Course he said to do it afore I got it half said. So Nick and I just collared everybody and herded 'em onto the railroad tracks. Down past where the depot is now. Well, we took them barrels and rolled 'em right down the tracks to where all the people were. And then when the fire came down there we just broke all them barrels with axes and pieces of railroad iron and anything we could get our hands on. And we poured that beer right off down the slope of the railroad grade where the fire was comin' right up through the grass toward the tracks. And that beer just drowned all that fire. Put it right out all along the tracks where the people were. Seemed like that fire backed right off from that beer. And so, there was me and Nick, standin' there watchin' the fire, and it agoin' off across the town, right away from the railroad. Didn't leave hardly anything. Swoopin' buildings up like they was only match boxes. Leavin' just a few houses and stores. And Nick Dodge's saloon. The fire just kind a jumped around the saloon. But the old depot, it went up in one blaze, seemed like. One big puff and that depot just wasn't there. That's the way all the buildin's went. One or two big whoopin' puffs, and they were gone. Hardly give a man time to see it. Not enough smoke to tell you which way the wind was blowin'. Just big flames, one after another, goin' up before you could blink and look at 'em twice. Before we knew it the whole town was practically gone, like as if it had never been here. And that's what me and Nick, and the people was alookin' at from there on the tracks above where we poured that beer out a all them there barrels."

Tobe's voice had become gradually deeper and slower before he stopped talking. He looked at two or three of the faces about him with eloquent finality. His face was a grinning, triumphant challenge. No one said anything for a few moments. Every face was fixed toward Tobe. He saw the shine of several pairs of eyes, and became apparently satisfied. His eyes dropped to the coal bucket, and his face became extremely solemn and grave.

"Well, what was we to do?" Tobe asked, in a low, helpless tone. "There was all them people bereften of all they had. Actin' like a bunch of children. A' cryin' and talkin' senseless. And some of 'em just starin', like they'd lost their voices as well as their senses. Well, me and Nick Dodge got together there on the tracks off away from the others, and then we started to figurin'. It would be a good two months afore snow'd fly, near as we could figure. We thought we'd ought to be able to do somethin'. Then I hit on an idea. Nick liked the idea right away. So, we just flagged the next freight. Big through train it was. He didn't like to stop, but he did. And we told him we wanted a few box cars. Three or four of 'em. We wanted them for the winter. We'd rent 'em, and Nick told him he'd pay what was reasonable. Nick's word was good as gold, and everybody knew him, even the railroad people. Well, the very next day in come them box cars. They dropped four of 'em in on the siding. We went to work on 'em right off. Partitioned them and made 'em tight and snug with grass and clay. Didn't take long, only about a week or two. We fixed up a couple of houses too, out of a lot of pieces we found after the fire. Not very good, but we made 'em tight with a lot of grass and clay. And then Nick, he took two families into the saloon. Anyways, we were all ready by the time frost came. And we got through the winter one way and another. Only a couple or three died. Sickly. Old people they were. Probably would a died anyway."

Tobe stopped, and looked down at the coal bucket as before. When Joker Harvey leaned over and hit the bucket with a little resounding splash, Tobe was not this time surprised at all. He didn't even seem to notice it. His little bony face was beaming now. He seemed to be looking at things more real than the coal bucket and its tobacco stains.

Tobe moved in his chair, shifting his chin in his overcoat collar. "Then," he said very abruptly, "in the spring we all pitched in. Got lumber from a mill down on the river. Nick Dodge got two span a mules. Started haulin' lumber from a mill down on the river. Then we went to buildin'. Built about a dozen houses, I reckon. Jesse Marsh even put up a grocery store. Even fixed up a school. A kind a side room on Jesse's store, it was. Jesse's wife taught there first, about six weeks every winter. And that's the way Prairie Green started up again. All brand new. Startin' up, before the fire'd cooled off hardly. That's the way we did things when Nick Dodge was here, runnin' his saloon down on the corner there. And me akeepin' bar for him till he up and died the year the grasshoppers came. And there ain't no man can as much as look at his shadder ever since. And that's what I know about Nick Dodge, and me his own barkeep that's sayin' it too."

Tobe Snow stood up slowly. He jabbed the pipe into his mouth, as if it had suddenly become hot in his hand. He glowered down at the faces about the stove, his brows arching slightly, as if he disdained to say another word. He stood more and more erect, drawing himself deliberately away from the men. At last, turning abruptly, he went off toward the front of the store, his gaze fixed as if on the very doorknob itself. As he went out into the whirling snow, he slammed the door behind him. His hat and shoulders showed dimly against the big plate-glass window, and then were gone.

II

Whenever Josh Bowdin was in the store, Tobe would be sure to tell the story about the famous set of whang harness. This was usually in late March, on one of those long wet nights when the winter was breaking up. Josh would always return to Prairie Green about this time, after a winter trip down to Missouri for mules, or sometimes to Texas after a few loads of steers. Tobe liked to see Josh back in town, though he never said as much to anybody, and least of all to Josh. Josh would always come back some day in March, wearing his corduroys and big boots, and his wide gray hat pushed far back on his head. And his big booming voice would fill the street, talking and laughing with the farmers and the men in the doorways of the stores. But Tobe would hardly pay attention to him. He would just walk on down the street, as if he wasn't interested. Tobe had heard the men around town talking about what he had once told Josh about the dry weather. As long as Prairie Green kept remembering that, Tobe wouldn't have to say much more to Josh Bowdin when he was on the street here the first day he was back from Missouri or Texas. He could just wait till evening. Josh would be sure to be in the hardware store the first night after he was back. And Tobe had never missed coming to the store the night after Josh came back from buying mules and steers.

The men would be there around the stove, listening to Josh's great rich voice and laughing with him about the way Missouri mules acted when you tried to get them into cattle cars. Tobe would always come in about nine o'clock. He would come all the way back through the store and sit down without saying anything, paying no attention to anybody, apparently not noticing Josh at all or hearing his talk or his laughter. The big grin would leave Josh's face. He would go on, talking very seriously now, almost solemnly, about contrary mules and wild Texas cattle. At last he'd get up, lean over the stove, and spit into the coal bucket. While settling back into his chair, he would look over at Tobe and with a slow smile, say, "Well, Tobe, glad to be back with you again." Josh would go on packing tobacco into a pipe then, the smile deepening into his lowered face. He was the only man in Prairie Green that dared to greet Tobe Snow like that.

Tobe, all the while gazing into the coal bucket, seemed hardly to have heard what Josh had said. Everyone was silent now. The men kept looking half-furtively at Tobe but nobody except Josh Bowdin was ever smiling openly. A sly twinkle seemed to be coming slowly into Tobe's abstracted eyes. At last the little black pipe came out of his mouth, and he began to speak down to the coal bucket, very deliberately and evenly, as if hardly caring whether the others heard him or not. His face seemed to be filled with complete disdain for everything except the coal bucket and his own thoughts. Only there was a peculiar tilt to Tobe's head tonight, a lighter movement of his bearded mouth and chin, and the slightest brightness in his gray watery eyes.

There was something gay about him as he started to speak, something which he was keeping to himself, hiding it behind his small withered face and under the deliberate evenness of his voice.

"You boys don't remember a span of mules that was once in this town," Tobe was saying. "None of you don't remember anything about 'em. They didn't come from Missouri either. Came from Ohio. Jack Bowdin brought 'em in here." Tobe never mentioned the fact that Jack Bowdin, one of his contemporaries, was Josh Bowdin's uncle. Josh and the younger generation never seemed to deserve such recognition. And as Tobe stopped for a moment, looking more intently before him, he seemed to be remembering things about Jack and the mules which it would be no use telling to the men about him, things that belonged to himself alone. His withered throat moved up and down for a few moments, like a man chuckling deep within himself, quite noiselessly.

"Well, them mules wasn't any bigger 'n oversize jackrabbits. They was thin, scrawny looking mules. Them stub tails a theirs looked almost as big around as their bellies. Everybody was laughin' at Jack Bowdin. Jack brought 'em in here for haulin' lumber for the new schoolhouse. Haulin' it from away down on the river. Mighty long hard haul, too. But Jack just let 'em laugh. He knowed what he was doin', gettin' them mules. They had big necks, and they was pullin' fools, that's what they was. Pullinest things I ever seed inside a set of tugs.

"Well, I was makin' harness then. Had my shop over where the postoffice is now. When I saw Jack takin' them mules out that first day, startin' for the river, I had to laugh. They didn't look no bigger 'n a couple a lean dogs, trottin' down the street in front of the long set of runnin' gears. Their harness lookin' like it was about four times too big for them. You'd just think every minute they'd step into their own collars and stumble down on top a themselves right there in the street. But there they went. Jack had brass mounted harness on them too, stickin' away up above 'em like poles. That was the way Jack was.

Ridin' along on the runnin' gears, standin' away up above the mules, payin' no attention to anybody.

"Then, it wasn't hardly noon yet, and Jack came back to town. But he didn't have a stick a lumber. Not a plank. He was walkin' behind the mules, not even any runnin' gears. He came around to the shop, drivin' the mules afoot. And what do you suppose it was? It was one of them mules' tugs. Snapped off as clean as you ever see. And Jack agrinnin'. Just agrinnin', and hardly sayin' anything. So I spliced the tug for him. Made it double. Took me half the afternoon. But I made it double, and stout as I could.

"The next day Jack went down to the river again. But about noon, here he comes again, without a plank of lumber, runnin' gears, or anything. Up to the shop he comes, and there was the other mule and his tug snapped in two clean as you please. And Jack grinnin' more 'n ever. Sayin' nothin', but just grinnin', and proud a them mules—so proud he'd have been willin' for 'em to tear their harness till there wouldn't have been two straps hangin' together. Several fellers from around town came down there. They couldn't believe their eyes. The same fellers that had been laughin' at Jack for gettin' the mules.

"So I said to Jack, just kind of jokin', I said, why don't you get a set of whang harness. You know what whang is. It ought to be tough enough. Of course I said it, never thinkin'. All the boys laughed, and looked at Jack.

"But Jack didn't laugh very much. Just kept grinnin' and lookin' at the mules. Then he looked down at the ground, and started to studyin', and still agrinnin'. After a while he looked up, and what'd he do but tell me to make the harness. Said that's just what he wanted. A set of whang harness. Of course we all laughed. But that didn't make no difference. He said that's what he wanted. Whang harness. At least whang tugs. And him still agrinnin', only kind of sly, and talkin' straight to me.

"I asked him if he knew what whang'd do when it got wet. I told him a set of whang tugs would stretch a mile. But that didn't make no difference at all. He only said he wanted whang and nothin' else. Sayin' it kind of sly, I thought. But sober as a judge.

"So I made the tugs for him. Half the boys in town comin' around and laughin' and watchin' me. Sewed 'em several thicknesses, tight as I could. Took me all that afternoon and part of the next mornin'. And so out goes Jack, him and the mules, and them new yaller tugs danglin' over their backs, almost adraggin' the ground. And everybody standin' around, laughin' and hollerin' at him. But him hardly payin' any attention at all. Keepin' things to himself, grinnin' just a little, almost as sober as the mules.

"Of course everybody waited to see what'd happen. They didn't know hardly what to look for. Some was sayin' he would make it. And some was sayin' he wouldn't. And some was talkin' about the bad place in the road out south a town. And some was lookin' at the sky just awishin' and ahopin' it'd rain.

"Well, sure enough, about four o'clock it did start rainin'. Clouded up in no time, without no warnin', just like it was watchin' the time and decidin' all at once. Got mighty dark. And then it came all of a sudden. Just pourin' down. Everybody standin' in the doors and lookin' out at it and grinnin'. Everybody in town talkin' about Jack Bowdin and them whang tugs.

"Well, it kept on rainin', it must have been about an hour. Everybody still astandin' along the street, back inside the open doors, just waitin'. Just waitin' and standin' there."

Tobe's voice had stopped abruptly and jerkily. His mouth remained slightly open, as if he had lost control of his voice. But something like a crafty smile came into the rest of his face. His eyes were sharp and observant as they went slowly and deliberately around the circle of faces beside the stove. His gaze fastened on Josh Bowdin.

Tobe got slowly up from his chair. The little black pipe was lifted before him, stiffly, in a gesture of suspense, the stem pointed at Josh. Tobe's watery eyes contracted to glittering beads as he looked down intently over his pipe, at Bowdin. The faint smile was now gone from

Tobe's face. He became very serious as he started speaking in a low, solemn tone.

"Then, what did we see?" Tobe stopped, and his eyes went slowly and rhetorically from face to face of the men beside the stove. He looked down at Josh Bowdin again. "What did we see, all at once, out there in the street? We seed Jack Bowdin and them mules, that's what we seed. And him awalkin' out aside the mules, drivin' 'em steady and slow right through the rain. But that was all, just Jack and them mules. Not a sign of any lumber, not a wagon wheel behind 'em."

After another short period of silence, Tobe went on, speaking now with an air of solemn mystery. "And next thing everybody knowed, the rain stopped. All at once, just like it begun. And there was Jack Bowdin and them mules up there in front of the school house, the mules leanin' into their collars a little, and Jack holdin' a steady line on 'em. And out behind 'em, there was them whang tugs, stretchin' all the way along the street, straight as a die clean out to, the end of town, and nobody knowin' how much further."

Tobe seemed to draw slightly back from the men in the chairs, then stood there watching them. He pulled his bent old body up to its full height. His small face seemed exultant, yet self-possessed. His thin brows were arched in suspense. His little eyes shone almost fiercely, yet secretly, mysteriously. Never had Tobe Snow seemed so eloquent, so unembarrassed, so sure of himself, as he waited now, looking steadily down at the men.

At last he dropped his head slightly, almost patronizingly. "Well," he said, "what do you suppose everybody did? They didn't do nothin', that's what they did. Just kept starin' and starin', like they was wonderin' whether to believe their eyes. Lookin' at Jack and them mules and them tugs stretchin' all the way back along the street.

"Then all at once, the sun came out. Come out strong, just blazin' down. Started dryin' things up. Just dried things up in no time. Pretty soon there wasn't even any mud left in the street. Then them whang tugs, they started to gettin' dry. Not so black and shiny like they was.

But gettin' yallower and yallower all the time. Then, just all at once they was dry. Then a course they started shortenin' up. Losin' their stretch and gettin' shorter and shorter. Then, sudden like, everybody heard it, away out at the edge of town. And the first thing everybody knowed, there it was comin' up the street. Jack Bowdin's wagon, all by itself, and a big load a lumber on it. It acomin' right straight up the street. Wabblin' a little, but pretty straight too, its spring tongue stayin' up stiff off the ground. It kept comin' and comin'.

It went all the way along the street, right on to where the mules and Jack was. Jack ran around and grabbed the tongue, and he steered it slap into the ring on the neckyoke. And there it was, that load of lumber, astandin' there beside where they was buildin' the school house. Right there in the street, real as daylight. A big whoppin' load too. And them mules out in front of it, not even breathin' hard. And there was Jack up on the wagon already, astartin' to unload that lumber."

Tobe Snow drew himself up, and looked down haughtily at the men in the chairs. Plainly, now, he was putting on a pose, and not trying to hide it. There was something purposeful and rhetorical about it. The faint crafty smile came back into his face. He leaned over slightly, his gaze fixed upon Josh Bowdin. "That there's how Jack Bowdin worked mules in the old days," he said, "And they wasn't Missouri mules neither." He added this with a sour grin. Now he looked down at the men in malevolent triumph. The crafty grin spread wide and tight across his small face as he withdrew his head slowly behind the collar of his old coat.

Tobe Snow turned and walked steadily toward the front of the store. The faces of all the silent men were lifted up from their chairs, to watch him. The bang of the front door came crashing back through the store. Tobe's face stopped and turned for a furtive moment at the plate-glass window, then disappeared in the darkness.

III

It was late April. Two nights before, thieves had come in a truck to the Widow Murphy's farm out south of town, and had boldly hauled twenty-two hogs out of a small rye field where they were pasturing. Since then it had been the whole talk of the town. The sheriff had been down from the county seat, and had left again for a small stockyards far down state, from which he had received a clue regarding the hogs. Rose Murphy had insisted on herself going with him and the deputy to identify the hogs. They had driven away only this morning, in the sheriff's Ford sedan.

There had been heavy rains, and an unusual number of farmers were in town this afternoon. Everywhere along the street, little groups of men were talking about the Widow Murphy's hogs.

Snow went along the sidewalk, seeming to pay no attention to all this. His small face under the old hat and his whole body appeared to be bent on something directly in front of him. He walked without the least appearance of hurry, but as with a deliberate, very fixed purpose. He was making his regular afternoon round, and was now on his way to the pump-house, to oil up the two big gas engines that would be forcing fresh water into the red tower tank during the early part of the night. Tobe seemed to hear none of the talk of the men as he went on down the sidewalk. When Josh Bowdin, from a larger group in front of the hardware store, saluted him heartily but respectfully, he hardly nodded. For the past two days Tobe had shown no signs of caring, or for that matter, of even knowing, anything about Rose Murphy's hogs.

Tobe had made only one comment on the whole affair. It had been a single curt remark, made under his breath, and strictly to himself. He had been going one of his rounds this morning, just as the sheriff and his deputy and Rosy Murphy were leaving town. He had seen them just as they pulled out of the gas station. He had seen the Widow Murphy sitting, rigid and vehement, in the back seat, her little black hat perched confidently on top of her head. Tobe had seen her just for a moment, in a single glance, as the Ford had turned into the street. He had said, simply, "That woman, atryin' to catch hog thieves!" Glowering after the car as it went out of the town, he had chuckled once or twice and then gone on down the street.

It was one of Tobe's philosophical habits never to have anything to do with women, especially never to listen to one of them talking. He had never heard Rose Murphy explain the motives of her life, as she had done repeatedly, to several men in the community. He did not know that she was simply trying to keep things about her place just the same as they had been when Michael J. Murphy was alive. He did not know Rose Murphy's unbounded respect for the dead. But it was not only because of this misunderstanding that he was entirely indifferent to all the talk of the men on the sidewalk this afternoon. Tobe Snow would also have his own inscrutable reasons. Evidently, he was simply biding his time to speak. Amidst all this hubbub he was keeping himself to himself, and his mouth shut, until Prairie Green would be rational and respectful enough to listen.

As the afternoon ended, the farmers drifted out of town, in their wagons and muddy Fords. Then the dusk came gradually. The street became silent. Talk seemed suspended everywhere. It was as if all Prairie Green had become hushed and expectant, waiting only for the news of Rose Murphy's hogs.

Not until darkness had come, and lights appeared here and there along the street, did men gather again to begin talking, slowly and quietly as if they must somehow beguile a long night of waiting.

The group in Allison's hardware store was unusually large tonight. Four or five farmers had straggled in, with tense, serious faces. J. P. Cass, the President of the super-annuated local Horse Thief Detective Association, was there, waiting for a wire from the sheriff. They were keeping the depot open tonight, to get the wire as soon as it came through. J. P. Cass owned a half section of the best land in the county, a few miles north of town. He had been county auditor once, about ten years ago. Before that he had been the township trustee for a long period. He was a man whose word had great weight in the whole community, and especially at times like this.

The talk in the store seemed slow and measured tonight. Every word was given thoughtful, deliberate emphasis. It wasn't merely that J. P. Cass, being there, made the men hesitate about saying too much, though they did look up intently whenever he spoke. But chiefly, everybody simply felt the seriousness of the matter. It was a time for few words and serious responsibility.

Joker Harvey, the butcher, half sitting against a roll of woven wire, had said something about them sending the thieves up for a good long term, twenty years or more—life, if he could have his way about it. Josh Bowdin was talking about the chances of identifying the hogs once they were mixed or scattered in any stock yards. This had a special interest for Josh, as a stock-buyer, and he talked across to J. P. Cass in a confidential though respectful tone. J. P. Cass, looking down at his toe, and then up toward the front of the store as if expecting somebody to arrive with the wire from the sheriff, and then back down at his toe, had only said, very solemnly and ominously, that if this kind of thing wasn't stopped right off, there was no telling where it would end. Herb Allison, the hardware merchant, floating here and there about the edges of the circle of men, had remarked two or three times about the boldness of it all. And one of the farmers had taken his hat off, rubbed his head, and said flatly that the two hands out at the Murphy place had been ready to remove the hogs from the rye field to a pasture beside the barn the very next day after the hogs were taken. Perry Lawson, the grain man, had spoken in his soft suave voice about how sorry he was to see the whole thing happen, and especially to a widow woman like Mrs. Murphy.

The door opened, and the men all looked toward the front of the store. It was Tobe Snow. As he came back through the store, there seemed to be something unusual about him. He wore the inevitable drooping hat and the same colorless overcoat pinned up close to his chin. His walk was slow and steady, and his head was dropped slightly as usual. But his watery eyes were looking very far out in front of him, at something of especial importance. Very plainly, he had this evening risen very far above such matters as the oiling of gas engines, or the stealing of the Widow Murphy's hogs. And he carried the little black pipe in his hand rather than in his mouth. It was the first time he had ever arrived in the store with the pipe in his hand. Half consciously, all the men noted this. It was a sign and a promise. Tobe Snow was to tell a thing tonight that had not escaped his lips for years.

Tobe sat down, amidst a short general silence, in a chair directly opposite to Josh Bowdin and J. P. Cass, from which he would be able to look at the faces of all the men. At first, however, he seemed hardly to note their presence. Instead, his small eyes were fixed immediately on the coal bucket. There was no fire now, in late April, and the coal bucket had become half filled with wads of tobacco-stained paper, bits of twine, cigar butts, and a few red and green tobacco cans. Tobe's mouth was sucked inward, in a way very unusual for him, until at last it became only a folded line across his face. It might have been a deliberate, half-disguised grin, and it might have been a sign of great philosophical concentration. Only his slightly shiny eyes revealed that he was absorbed in matters infinitely more important than coal buckets or what the men around him might be talking about.

It was Josh Bowdin who started the talk again. He said something about the difficulty of identifying stolen hogs. The others went on, speaking from time to time, slowly and hesitantly as before. They kept looking at Tobe now and then, vaguely conscious of something unusual in him. He seemed especially indifferent to them and their talk tonight. Only once did he look up from the coal bucket. It was just after Perry Lawson had said again how sorry he was that it had to be the Widow Murphy. Tobe's eyes stared at the man in a quick look of disdain. A moment later he went back to the coal bucket as if for relief.

It was nearly an hour later before Tobe first spoke. The talk had died down to mere fragmentary remarks. And now there was a long silence. Tobe's eyes blinked, lifted from the coal bucket, and went slowly around the circle of faces. He saw that Prairie Green had grown tired of its idle talk at last. He shifted upward in his chair. All the men looked at him with curious, expectant eyes. His gaze fastened on J. P. Cass and Josh Bowdin. His folded mouth opened and he began to speak. His voice sounded like a sudden, resentful cackle breaking above the absolute silence in the store.

"It was just after they opened up the first livery barn here," he said abstractedly, as if linking his words with something that had gone before in his mind. "They wasn't many rigs in the whole country yet. Pete Zellers, he had the finest. Brand new. Flashin' yaller wheels, and all the trimmin's. Real leather seat, fancy top. Pete, he lived just this side a the river. Big fine farm down there. You fellers don't remember anything about Pete. Shame he got started playin' the Board a Trade. Went busted. Then dug out. Don't know where he went."

Tobe's eyes had dropped to the toe of his oversized shoe. He looked at his foot more and more complacently as his voice went on. But now his eyes darted around the faces of the men. He saw Josh Bowdin also looking at the shoe. A flash of resentment seemed to come from his eyes, as if Josh had no right to be interested in the shoe. Then his gaze dropped again. The suggestion of a wary smile came back into his face. He seemed to be finding his own secrets again, hidden somehow in the big scuffed toe.

"Pete had a team of sorrel horses. Fastest flesh ever I seed in this country. Decked out all fancy. Brass mounted harness. I made them harness. Spent most of a whole winter on 'em. They was the kind of harness you'd like to see on horses like them was.

"Well, Pete used to come into town like the wind. Sittin' up in that flashin' new buggy, drivin' like mad. Keepin' a stiff line on that team till he got right up to the hitch rack in the street. And always holdin' a whip over 'em. Not that he needed to, with them sorrels. But Pete was that way. He'd hold a whip over anything he drove. Pete was a hard man some ways. Most fellers didn't like him. It was like he was holdin' a whip, when he talked to people. Only me and Pete always got along fine. It was just the way he had. Makin' them harness for him, me and Pete got along fine.

"One day word came into town about them sorrels of Pete's. Jack Bowdin heard about it first. He was workin' at the livery stable then. It was before Jack got his mules. Jack came runnin' up to the harness shop. Told me Pete's sorrels were stolen. He was just shoutin'. Wanted me to go right down there with him. So we took the best team they was in the livery stable. Was out of town in no time. Everybody else just standin' around, talkin' crazy excited. That's all they was doin' all over town.

"We drove right down to Pete's place. Pete wasn't there. Was over the other side of the river, pickin' out timber he was goin' to use for some buildin'. It was one of the hired men had come into town to tell about the stealing. Come in on an old slow work mare Pete had.

"Well, we got there, and fast too. Had a good team of big bays afore us. But we couldn't find out nothin'. Hired men just knew Pete's sorrels were gone, that's all. They'd been out in the field when it happened. The women folks so excited they couldn't tell us anything certain. Just plumb 'istorical, they was. One said they'd taken the sorrels towards the river. The other said the other way. One said they was two men with shotguns. Other said it was just one man, said he had a pistol and a shotgun both.

"Jack and me had to figure it out for ourselves. We figured they'd take the road to the river, then follow the trail road. They wasn't any towns on the trail road for a long ways. They'd probably cross at the bridge down this side of Wayneton. Then try to get away to the southern part of the state. Takin' a road through the hills, drivin' at night, hidin' in the daytime. They wasn't hardly any towns to mention on them hill roads neither.

"We drove hard for the river. Knew we couldn't hope to catch 'em for a day or two. Mebbe a week. But wanted to keep close right at the start. It'd help to trace 'em easier. Down at the river we thought we seed their tracks. Couldn't be sure, but looked like it just when we turned into the old trail road.

"We was goin' along the trail road. A little slower. Had to pull up a little on account of the road. Then Jack asked all at once, a cold steady look comin' in his eye, he asked who'd I think it was. Course I didn't know nothin' about horse thieves. Jack did, workin' in the livery barn that way, hearin' fellers talkin'. He said he was sure it was nobody but Nig Harper hisself. Just about the worst horsethief ever untied a halter in this whole country. Jack said he was sure it was him. Pickin' the best team in the whole country like that. Just comin' in and doin' the job in the daytime that way. Looked like Harper, Jack said. Nobody else. And then Jack laughed a little. He was thinkin' of what the women said. Seein' two men and then seein' one man, and not knowin' which way they went off. Jack knew what women was when it came to things like that. Horse stealin'...or any kind of stealin'."

Tobe's high crackling voice stopped deliberately. He looked over at J. P. Cass, then at the other men, his face filling with scorn and disgust for a half-minute or more. It was as close as he would come to any mention of the Widow Murphy or her hogs.

His voice rose again. He spoke resentfully and very laconically for a while. "We kept on. Crossed at the Wayneton Bridge about four o'clock. Pulled up into the hills. The road kept windin' around like a snake full a whiskey. Couldn't see nothin' ahead. Didn't meet nobody anywheres. They was a little ol' house at one place. Only an ol' woman there. Couldn't tell us nothin', got all excited. Couldn't a told which way the rig was goin' if she had seed it.

"We kept goin' on till dusk. The road got pretty dark. Then, about nine o'clock we got a moon. That made it easy. Your eyes gettin' more and more used to lookin' ahead, you could see as plain as day. Course I was carryin' one a the shotguns all ready then. Keepin' it between my knees. Huntin' a man like Nig Harper, you had to be fixed for him any time.

"We kept goin' that way all that first night. Jack's bays was a big powerful team. Pulled them hills steady all night. Hardly stopped once. Give 'em a breath or two just a few times after bad places in the road on sides a long hills.

"Well, about mornin' we got to a little place. Just a few houses. Looked like boxes settin' together at the bottom of a hill. Settin' there very still, and it kind of dark yet all around 'em. Found one old feller there. Putterin' around, lightin' a lamp in just a little two-by-four store. Course he didn't know nothin'. Pretty soon some other fellers came in from the houses. They talked enough, but didn't say nothin'. One feller said he thought he'd heard a rig goin' by in the night. But the others looked at him only like he had no business talkin' at all. He was a little feller with a funny lookin' head. You could tell he was a kind of halfwit.

"It was gettin' a little more light then. We started to lookin' around. Down at the end of the houses where the road turned, we found what we was lookin' for. They was buggy tracks there, fresh as you'd want to see. I saw Jack grinnin' at me then, there in the risin' light. The cold look comin' in his eyes, but him agrinnin' just the same. Jack was the quietest feller you ever see, in some ways. But he wasn't afeared a nothin'. And they wasn't anything he hated like horsethieves. He'd gone after the devil turned horsethief. That's what Jack would.

"We figured it wasn't any use agoin' right away. They wouldn't be drivin' them sorrels in the daytime. They'd hide out somewheres in the hills till night. We'd just have to wait. Might see where their tracks left the road. And then, we mightn't. The road was pretty muddy in places, and sometimes it was just bare rock on the sides a hills. We'd just have to wait till night. Couldn't risk gettin' ahead of 'em. Fed and watered the team—had some corn in the back of the buggy. Got a bed from a feller in one of the houses. Slept there that day. His women folks didn't want us to...they was scared to death. Got all excited. You'd think we was the horsethieves ourselves. That's women folks for ye."

Tobe Snow stopped long enough to look at the men about him. The scorn came back to his face. The figure of Rosy Murphy came back to the minds of all the men in the store. Her spirit was there above them for a few moments, ridiculous and remote. Then Tobe's gaze went back to the solemn importance of his toe again.

"The next night we drove till daylight. Stoppin' only a couple times, when we thought we heard buggy wheels ahead of us. But they wasn't nothin'. Didn't see a thing. It was just sun-up when we got to Jay's Gap. Just a little place between two hills, no more than a' dozen houses. The road ran right through there. Some of them said they was sure they heard a team goin' through in the night. Three or four fellers said they did. But you couldn't be sure. They was talkin' big. Wanted to seem important. You could tell that. The road all along there was hard and rocky. You couldn't tell anything about tracks. Anyways we stayed. Didn't go on another foot. Just waited till night again. We couldn't be goin' wrong. We was pretty sure a that. Not any other road to speak of in that whole country. Jack was sure of it. His look just as cold as ever. Him just grinnin'—sure, like a feller already lookin' over his head and seein' the eyes of his man plain as day.

"Well, we kept that up for four days. Sleepin' in the daytime. Drivin' hard every night, clear till mornin'. We kept findin' their tracks ever' day. We got away down in them hills. Found out afterwards it was almost the state line. About twenty miles from Williamsville. Big town in them days. Mills there on the river. Boats came in there then. But we didn't know. Didn't know where we was exactly. Only, we was sure that road couldn't go on much further in them hills. Knew it'd be gettin' out somewhere pretty soon. Hittin' towns somewhere. And that's what we was afraid of. They'd keep shy of towns, certain. Pull off somewheres. Keepin' away from towns. And then we'd lose 'em. Only, we knowed one thing certain. We'd gone clean to creation away from everywhere, follerin' that road through them hills."

One of the farmers in the store suddenly broke in upon Tobe. He asked, very abruptly, "How far away was you from here?" The farmer was a little man with a red over-eager face. He had never heard Tobe Snow talking before. Josh Bowdin looked at him with a cautioning leer. Tobe only lifted his eyes from his foot and stared resentfully at the little man. After a long moment or two his eyes dropped again, and he went on as if he had never been interrupted.

"The fourth night, just comin' daylight, all at once there they was. We seed 'em, but they never seed us. Seed 'em just plain enough to tell. They was apullin' off the road into a kind of gully at the bottom of a hill. It was thick timber down in there. But we knowed what they was doin'. Goin' to hide out somewheres down in that timber till the next night. Jack was for goin' right down there at first. Goin' right down there and shootin' it out with 'em. But I told him no. I had another way, a whole lot surer. After awhile Jack agreed. So we just pulled off into the timber on the other side of the road. Got the team away back from the road, in behind a big pile of rock and bushes.

"We waited there all day. Nothin' to eat, not even any water for the team. Couldn't move even to feed the team. Just kept watchin' ever' second through the bushes.

"What we figured was we'd wait till just before night. Then we'd slip back to the road with the shotguns. They was a big rock just beside the gully, right where they'd have to come out into the road. We'd get behind that, and cover 'em with the shotguns just when they came into the road. Cover 'em that way afore they'd have time to wink, afore they could even breathe.

"Soon as dusk came we went down there, keepin' behind trees, goin' quiet as we could. Got down to the road and behind that rock. It was good light yet. You could see all right. Didn't have to wait long. Heard 'em comin' up through the gully. Came right up to the rock. So close you could hear the wheel scrape. Then they stopped, to look into the road. Right then Jack told 'em what to do with their hands. We had 'em covered cold. Our guns right up almost in the buggy. Well, you'd never think they'd tried a thing, covered like that. But they did. The one that wasn't drivin' tried to get Jack. But Jack didn't even know his trigger arm had a hole in it till afterward. We got 'em both then. Plugged both their right shoulders. One of 'em tried to jump. Fell in the wheel. The other dropped down into the bottom of the buggy. Jack had the lines by that time, afore one of them horses moved a muscle. Had that team pulled over and wedged in between two trees. They hadn't gone twenty feet afore he had 'em quiet as two kittens and tied up to them trees with the reins. The feller in the bottom of the buggy was groanin'. The other was back in the road, all bloody, and he wasn't stirrin'. I was holdin' the gun on 'em. You couldn't take no chances.

"Jack came back and looked at 'em. They wasn't dead, not even the feller in the road. But they looked like they was done up. There was a puddle of blood under the feller in the bottom of the buggy, and the road was all shiny red around where the other feller was layin'. Kind a sickly sight. But we had to do it. They'd a plugged us if we didn't get 'em first.

"We stuffed a couple bandanna handkerchiefs in where the shots had got 'em. Then found some old towels around some bread and pork they had in the back of the buggy. Used them too. That way we got the blood kind a stopped. After a while they didn't bleed near so much. We got 'em up into the buggy then. Jack tied 'em in the seat, both of 'em. Wouldn't take no chances at all. Then I fixed up Jack's arm. He didn't hardly want to pay any attention to it. But I made him. Fixed it up with one of them towels. Tyin' it real tight till the bleedin' stopped.

"Then Jack just stood there lookin' up at them fellers, and still grinnin', and that cold look still in his eyes. Jack wasn't such a hard man exackly. It wasn't that he liked to see 'em shot up. He was just feelin' so good, a catchin' them horse thieves. That was all.

"Jack wanted me to take the team and the two fellers and go on ahead. He'd come behind with the other team and keep watchin'. If them fellers came to and tried anything he'd be ready for 'em. Jack wouldn't risk nothin'. Them seemin' like they was done up even. Layin' up there in the buggy white as death exceptin' for the blood smears.

"Well, I got in, turned the team around, started away slow. I'd let Jack come on behind. Never dreamed a what'd happen. Then just a few minutes and I heard wheels. Didn't even look back. Just supposed it was Jack. Then the first thing I knowed I heard a shot. Came singin' right through the buggy top. The team was off, and I let 'em go, just managin' to see back at what it was. They was two fellers and a team. A good way back, but comin' right for me. One of 'em standin' up and whippin'. The other sittin' back and tryin' to get his gun on me. Didn't know what to think at first. Fact, wasn't any time for thinkin'. Just gettin' away. Drivin', and drivin' hard, that's what I had to do. I seed that, in a jiffy.

"Well, I got away all right. Wasn't any horse flesh goin' to catch me with Pete Zellers' team in front of me. It was pretty hard though. Them two fellers piled up in the seat there with me. Me with one foot out on the step, tryin' to drive that way. But I did it. Pulled right away from that team back there.

"Come to a bad place in the road, though. Down between two hills. The other team kind a caught up a little. They started shootin' again, but pretty wild. Only once, it wasn't so wild. One of the shots splintered a buggy spoke under me.

"But I made it. Got up where the road was leveler, and pulled right off from 'em again. About that time I heard shots away behind. Looked back, and there was Jack, comin' down that hill, drivin' like mad. He started lettin' go at them fellers, and them tryin' to get through the bad place in the road. I got my team stopped then. We had 'em between us then, down in that holler. I started crankin' at 'em too, out a the back of the buggy, and tryin to hold my team the same time. Jack and me both pepperin' 'em that way, they stopped. Standin' up in their rig, holdin' their hands up. Looked mighty funny, they did. One of 'em tryin' to hold his mitts away up and hold the team too. We quit shootin' then. But Jack came on. Came up behind their rig down there in the holler. I could hear him shoutin' at 'em. Then he was drivin' 'em right afore him, all the way across the holler. Brought 'em right up to where I was. Jack made 'em stop there, and drove up beside 'em. They was the funniest lookin' pair you'd ever see. One of 'em was pretty big and dark, and he'd lost his hat. The other was a little fat feller. They was just shakin' like leafs. Standin' there in the buggy with their mitts away up as high as they could stretch 'em, and shakin' like leafs.

"They was ashakin' so they couldn't hardly talk. But after a while we found out who they was. The big dark feller was a sheriff. The little fat one was a deppity. They'd come up from Williamsville. The word had got down there about the horse stealin', and the team goin' that way. And they'd come up to head 'em off. They thought I was the thief, tryin' to turn back and get away from 'em. We got 'em quieted down then. Told 'em who we was. But they didn't laugh a bit. Just sittin' there now, ashakin'. Couldn't say nothin' hardly. After a while they got turned around though. Started on back toward Williamsville, Jack and me watchin' 'em. We just had to laugh. We knowed what they was after. They was after a reward. Thought they'd stop the thieves out here in the hills, and get the reward all for themselves. It was pretty funny, seein' 'em go off down through that holler again, drivin' slow, tryin' to dodge rocks and holes.

"Well, we got started on then, me goin' on ahead, Jack keepin' close behind all the time. The two fellers I had in the buggy with me looked kind a different now. One of 'em would come to some, after all the holtin'. The other didn't look so dead either like he did at first. I kept watchin' 'em right along. They was all right, I knowed, tied into the rig like they was. But Jack kept right behind. Jack was sure not goin' to take no chances.

"Took us about two days comin' back. Stopped for a few hours at one of the places where we'd stayed before. Got some rest and somethin' to eat. Washed up the two fellers we'd caught. They kept lookin' stronger after they got somethin' to eat and drink. Gave 'em both a good shot a whiskey.

"We didn't have no trouble then. Kept drivin' steady all the way back. One of the fellers I had in the rig with me got so he could talk.

Talkin' wild, out of his head for a long time. Then, afore we got here, he was so he knew what he was sayin'. Gave me and Jack one of the best cussin's I ever heard. The other one just kept wakin' up once in a while and lookin' steady out in front of him. He didn't know nothin' though. Couldn't talk at all.

"Got back here to Prairie Green early in the mornin'. Just about daylight. Put the two fellers in ol' Doc Slack's office, up above the grocery store. Had to call Doc out of bed for it. Didn't even bother about Jud Marsh. He was marshal then. Wasn't no good tryin' to call him. He'd been asleep down in the office at the livery barn. Always sleepin' down there. Didn't know nothin'. Might just as well not been any marshal in town. Wasn't no good for nothin'.

"Well, everybody woke up that mornin', and there was the horse thieves, right there in Doc Slack's office. And Pete Zellers' team was there in the livery barn, real as any horse flesh this town ever seed. The fellers around town couldn't hardly believe their eyes. Just kept agoin' up to Doc's office to see them two fellers, and then down to the livery barn to look at the team. Asking me and Jack questions, the whole town talking at once and askin' questions. Of course we didn't try to tell 'em everything then. Didn't say much at all. Jack just sent word to Pete Zellers, tellin' him his team was up here in the livery barn. 'Nother feller drove over to the county seat. Left word at the sheriff's office.

"Then two fellers came here from over in the eastern part of the state. I forget, some big town over there. They was detectives. They knowed right off who them two horse-thieves was. It was just as Jack Bowdin said. We'd catched one a the worst horse thieves ever came into the state. Yes sir, nobody but Nig Harper. And the other one was a bad egg too. His name was Sanders. He'd been in the pen twice. Been mixed up in a lot a horse stealin' afore this. Yes sir, that's who we'd catched. Nig Harper and this feller Sanders. Nobody else.

"Well, must a been a month afore the trial came. Them two fellers was about all right then. We just told what happened, that was all. Me and Jack. But the Judge, he gave us a great speech. Talked about what we'd done for law and order. Me and Jack, we just listened, not sayin' anything. Didn't mind it much. The way Jack said afterward, me and him talkin' by ourselves, he was satisfied. Catchin' them horse thieves, that was all he wanted. Especially when it was Nig Harper. Jack hated horse thieves worse than anything. Dead against 'em. Jack told me once, he'd take a rattlesnake afore he would a horse thief."

A tone of solemn finality had come into Tobias Snow's voice. His mouth closed very slowly and very firmly, as if he were resolved never to open it again. He rose from the chair deliberately, like a man satisfied that he could now afford to keep still forever.

But after a few moments Tobe's eyes brightened, he leaned forward slightly as he stood gazing down at the faces of the men, and spoke again, with unmistakable condescension. He said, "That's how we used to catch thieves in this town—horse thieves." Then his whole face seemed to beam with scorn. He added, "And we didn't need no women to help us neither."

Tobias Snow turned and walked steadily out of the store. The door slammed behind him. The men about the stove looked at each other smiling. But nobody laughed aloud, and nobody said anything for some time.

Outside, the scuffling of oversized shoes moved along the street. It seemed to be the only sound in Prairie Green. The low dark stores pushed out over the sidewalk, listening curiously, but only the large white stars of April, which knew all things, even to such trifling matters as the exact whereabouts of Rosy Murphy's hogs, saw whether Tobe Snow's face was serious or grinning as he walked on steadily through the shadows in the street.

4.

AFTER CORNHUSKING

His wrist, bare between his leather mitten and the dirty sleeve of his sheepskin, ached slightly with the cold as it rested for an instant on the frosty edge of the barn door. He lifted the latch and went into the early morning dimness of the feedway. Old Kate stirred in her stall and whinnied softly, stretching toward him with her big breast pressing, against the oaken manger. The great bay horse beside her began to paw in the stall and to shake his bald face over the feed box.

Milton Kuthe scooped up the cobs from the boxes, flinging them behind him out of the feedway, feeling moist nostrils nuzzling at his wrists each time his hands dipped into the boxes. Then he went along the dark feedway toward the small crib at the rear of the barn, wading knee deep through some piles of straw.

When he opened the rickety crib door he smelt the sweet, raw odor of the "new corn," which he had scooped into the crib only a week ago. A heavy ear came thudding down the long slope of the corn, and he heard the crisp rustle of a husk at his feet. As he knelt slowly upon the corn he felt the ears hard and big under his knees. He began to pile some of the ears into the crook of his left arm, peeling the ribbony shucks from them with fumbling mittens.

As he came along the feedway the horses again began to paw and to whinny eagerly. As soon as he dropped the corn into the feed boxes he could hear the horses' teeth tearing the grain from the cobs. He lifted a long-handled fork out of a dark corner and carried big bundles of straw from the rear of the feedway. He noticed a slight sudden burnish upon the straw as he lifted each forkful into the manger.

After putting the fork down, Kuthe leaned his big body against the jamb of the feedway door. A soft diffused grayness was spreading over the barnlot outside. Everything was very still. He could hear only the crunching of corn behind him, loud and hollow in the horses' boxes.

Outside, the grayness became brighter. He could hear the crowing of a cock far away on the prairie. A faint, distant voice was calling hogs to an early feeding. He thought he could just hear the thin whanging of a scoop shovel flinging corn from a wagon.

Then he could hear no sound anywhere on the prairie. He looked quietly away at the hills far off to the east, low and gently rolling one into another, distinct now against a gray sky. The farthest and longest of the hills pushed its great smooth dome above the others. He could just see the posts, tiny and black, of a fence that wandered along the slope of this largest hill.

The hills became very distant, unreal. His gaze returned to the cornfields that stretched, almost unbroken, across the prairie. There was no rustling in the corn now. No banging of knockboards all about him in a frosty field. He remembered the tugging rhythm, at his shoulders, in the muscles of his arms—the laborious rhythm of the husking that had grown so monotonous during the long weeks of the fall. An aching tiredness came back for a moment into his hands, and he could feel the wet, cold husking mittens on his fingers, and the hardness of the husking hook against the butt of his thumb. He remembered the lurch and clatter of his wagon moving through the corn beside him, and the turning of its great mud-laden wheels. Then, suddenly the images of the husking left his mind. He gazed absently at the rows of broken stalks where the wagons had gone through the fields, and his glance fell upon the white insides of open husks clinging to some of the nearer stalks. But farther away the fields were to him only a blur of dull yellow, and farther still, only a grayish veil that drifted toward the hills, rather a vision in his mind than anything real in the world beyond him.

He stood for a long time vaguely looking over the cornfields. Very slowly he began to awaken from the stillness that had crept into his mind like a dream. He heard the big bay horse blowing and snorting softly in the manger behind him, and he was aware of the musty smell of fine straw dust in the air. He turned and saw the black lips of the horse tossing little sprays of straw over the top of the manger into the feedway. He reached over the manger and began to rub the white spot on the horse's head with his mittened hand. The animal was quiet for a moment, then went on pushing the straw out of the manger.

He stepped out of the feedway, turned and fastened the door behind him, then walked slowly across the farmlot toward a little white house that stood beside a bleak iron windmill. A tendril of blue smoke was creeping along the gray shingled roof, clinging to the eaves for a moment, then uncurling downward before it disappeared. As he walked on, he removed, the mittens from his hands and began to pick bits of straw out of the lining of the wristbands. He noticed some small white hairs on the palm of one of his mittens, but he did not try to remove these.

5.

POSSESSION

Wynne Snyder's heart was narrow like his house and deep like the old well on his lawn, and he kept the things he cherished at its very bottom. No one ever guessed by half how much he loved his black land, upon which he raised better corn and wheat than could be found anywhere else in the county. He was proud of his tall white house, with its long low porch and its pane of colored glass in the front door. And as for his huge, paintless barn, it almost seemed that he loved it better than the light of day, for it stood to the westward of his orchard, blotting out the sunset and keeping the evening light from ever pouring its red glory through the long rows of apple trees.

But if he found a dumb, unlimited satisfaction in all his chattels, there was another treasure more deeply hoarded in his heart, and more precious still. Nettie Snyder, his little hard-working wife, was more necessary to him than even his barn and his cattle.

He had got Nettie over beyond the Creek. She was the daughter of old Josh Griffin, the hardest man in that country to deal with. When he used to go over to old Josh's to buy yearlings, he would always go early, and take a lunch with him, for he knew it would take most of the day to make the deal. Old Griffin seemed to hate to sell a horse or a drove of yearlings, even when you knew he was ready to take your price. But on one of these occasions the old man was away from home, and his Missus invited the visitor to stay to dinner—old Mrs. Griffin was the very opposite of Josh, in everything. And that day Snyder met Nettie Griffin, who served him at dinner with sugar-cured pork and some very good crulls and coffee. Six months later Wynne Snyder and Nettie Griffin were married, after a long bitter struggle with her father, too long and bitter to describe, except to say that on the day of the wedding old Josh remained out of the house, dehorning some steers in one of the cattle sheds back of his barn. But it was just because the winning of her was such a difficult business that Wynne Snyder had come to care so much as he did for his wife. This was always the way with him. The pieces of land, the droves of cattle, the horses he had greatest difficulty in buying were those for which he always cared most.

But this was not the only reason why he cherished her so much. No man ever got a better housewife than Wynne Snyder. Nettie Griffin had learned from her mother how to bake bread the loaves of which looked and tasted, when they were still warm from the oven, almost like big toasted marshmallows. Her fried potatoes were crisp, with never a slice of them black or hard. Her crab and grape jellies, and her preserves of wild berries, were the envy of neighbor women. She could strip a cow as quickly as any hand her husband had ever had on the place. And she knew just how deep to sink the ring in a hog's nose, without touching the gristle.

With all the hardness and strength of her little hands, and the wrinkles, like little cobwebs, about her two small eyes, and her flat breasts, and her dirty unfastened shoes, she was Wynne Snyder's constant helpmate. She planned with him, when to buy more land, when to sell the corn and the cattle, helped him to calculate his taxes, advised him about his health, cared for his rheumatism, made his shirts, bought most of his clothes, cut his hair when he got older and hated the waits in the barber shop down in Kottsville. She served him almost like a slave and obeyed him like a child, yet ruled him as only a woman can rule her strong mate. It was from her that Wynne

Snyder drew, without knowing it, most of his confident, indomitable strength.

But no one would have guessed anything of this, to see him out in that other world he also lived in, among his men on the farm, with his neighbors on the street in Kottsville, or talking to farmers around the little red-bellied stove in Sam Kellogg's hardware store; to hear him buying young cattle from the little farmers over beyond the Creek without getting off his horse and with his shiny cattle whip drooping from his saddle horn. Everyone knew Wynne Snyder for a brisk trader, a big successful grain-grower and cattleman. There was even a swagger in his voice whenever he came home from Kansas City after selling a profitable drove of Shorthorns. To anyone with an eye for his neighbor's ways, it was plain what things ruled this man's life. And yet, no one around Kottsville ever fully realized how dear to him were his black land and his cattle. And no one ever guessed how much treasure his heart placed upon his hard-working little housewife. Most of the neighbors would have supposed only that she was a little more valuable to him, because a little more helpful, than the big bay mare which he always rode.

But at last a night came in the late April of 1895, and Nettie Snyder was found dead in her kitchen. The doctor said it was heart. But the neighbors said it was simply that she had worked herself to death; went down hitched to the plow, the men said; died over her own stove, the women said. As Mrs. Ormsbee told Len Ormsbee when he brought the news home from town, dyin' like that weren't the proper way for humans to be taken, especially since Nettie Snyder had the deepest feather beds of any woman in the country. But several neighbors went over to the Snyder place as soon as they heard it, to see what they could do. And some of the closer neighbors took charge of things, for they supposed Wynne would be a little upset and wouldn't care to be tending to things as usual.

When Bert Wilkins drove up to the gate he noticed that Len Ormsbee and the two Welt boys were already doing up the chores.

Bert said to his wife, "You can just go on in, Cary. I'll help get ever'thing fixed up for the evening out around the barn."

"Ain't you comin' in first, Bert? Just for a few minutes?"

"No, I'll just help with the feedin'. Reckon I couldn't do anything in there now, nohow. You just go on in, Cary."

In the house Mrs. Len Ormsbee and one of the Welt women were in the front bedroom with the undertaker, and the other Welt woman was tidying up the parlor. Cary Wilkins helped Mrs. Welt with the parlor, and then the two went out to the kitchen. It would be a good thing to boil some coffee and get a bite for everyone. Over the stove the two women began to talk, although they had said very little to each other in the parlor.

"You say he's been in there around the door ever since you come?" Mrs. Wilkins asked.

"Yes, they won't let him in the room where she is, you know. The undertaker said it'd be better to keep him out of there for a while, so Mrs. Ormsbee got the door locked. And he just stays outside there. Looks at you kind of strange whenever you pass him. But doesn't say anything. Only thing he said since we come was, 'You leave her alone.' Told us that when we started to take her out of the kitchen here where she was, to put her on her bed in there in the front room. Strange, the way he said it. Said, 'You folks just leave her alone. She don't belong to you,' he said. 'You leave her alone.' But of course the undertaker made out as if he didn't hear him, and we carried her right on in to the bedroom."

The kitchen door opened, and Wilkins came in, followed by the two Welt men. After a moment or two, Wilkins asked, "Where's Wynne? In where she is?"

The Welt woman told him where he was, and said she thought they had better get him out into the dining room pretty soon. The three men all said it would be better, they thought. Then the Welt woman and Bert Wilkins went on in toward the bedroom.

"Wynne, don't you think you'd better come on out in the dining room for a while?" Wilkins said as they approached the bedroom door. "There's some coffee out there the women have made. You'd better come on out there now, and have a cup of coffee."

The tall man standing beside the door moved slightly away from them, and they noticed that his hand was on the knob. His eyes looked like those of a mare in her stall, when her colt is dead at her feet.

After a little while Bert Wilkins said, "Wynne, you just kind of got to take ahold of yourself. You can't be goin' on like this."

The man standing at the door remained silent, looking at them with a frightened stare. He was shaking, and his overalls were fluttering up and down his legs as if he were standing in a gentle wind. Once he glanced nervously over his shoulder toward the closed room behind him, and a strand of grayish hair fell down over his prominent brown forehead, below which his eyes shone wildly and excitedly like those of a prodded beast. Suddenly he said, "You had all better get out of here. You ain't got no right to Nettie. You got to go away from here." Wilkins motioned to the Welt woman and they both went slowly back to the kitchen.

A little while later Len Ormsbee came in, after finishing the milking that Nettie Snyder had always helped the hired men to do. Then the undertaker and Mrs. Ormsbee and the other Welt woman came out into the kitchen from the bedroom. Bert asked them what Wynne was doing when they came out, and they said he was in the room now, standing beside the bed. They waited for a few minutes, and then Len Ormsbee went in to the bedroom alone. Len said maybe he could talk to him.

When he returned to the kitchen he said that Wynne was still standing beside the bed, but wouldn't say anything. Just standing there, staring down at the body.

Then someone said Wynne wouldn't be able, of course, the way he was acting, to arrange things at all, and they'd better kind of plan about the funeral. Len Ormsbee thought the sooner they got it over the better it would be for Wynne's sake. The elder of the Welt men said it was a busy season anyhow, and folks would find things kind of hard if it was held over too long. Bert Wilkins wondered why it couldn't be tomorrow just as well as not, and everybody agreed with him. The undertaker said that was kind of short, but he guessed it could be managed.

The undertaker went away, and Mrs. Wilkins and one of the Welt women said they would have to go home to their children for the night. The others decided to remain. "We'd better stay, as many of us as can," Ormsby had said; "it'll be better for some of us to be around, I think."

Snyder had finally come out from the bedroom, and one of the women had thought she heard him leaving the house by the dining room door. Bert Wilkins had said, after some time, "Wonder what he could be doing outside so long."

The younger Welt woman was sitting in a corner of the parlor, facing the door that came in from the dining room, and she could see beyond into the kitchen. Suddenly she screamed slightly, then sat stone-still in her chair, staring through the dining room door. In a moment Wynne Snyder was standing in the door, a rusty shotgun in his hands. For a good minute there was no sound or movement anywhere in the room. Snyder's long crooked thumb began to move, like a brown, awkward snake, down the stock of the gun, reaching slowly for the hammers. The two black hammers seemed to grow largely, grotesquely, incredibly large, as the man's thumb moved toward them. Then a dull click, followed by another dull click, broke the complete silence.

But the barrel of the shotgun kept pointing at a big red flower in the carpet. Wynne Snyder stood there, absolutely motionless, vaguely staring at the faces before him. At last he said, fiercely and suddenly, but quietly, "You have all got to go away. You ain't got no right here. You go away."

Ormsbee and the other men rose slowly from their chairs, watching the man with unblinking eyes. Ormsby glanced toward the women, and they hurried behind Welt's big body from the room. The men followed, and they and the women went through the front hall door out of the house. It was dark on the lawn, and only a small fragment of summer moon was hanging in the sky. It was Welt's hoarse voice that first spoke, "Better stay here in the yard, hadn't we?"

"No, no, you come home," his wife said, nervously pulling at his hand.

"No, won't do much good to stay," Ormsbee thought. "Might even make him worse if he saw us anywhere around." They started for the lawn gate. "We can't do anything now. Just have to wait till morning. Maybe he'll be a little different then."

After driving for a quarter of a mile or more, Ormsbee suddenly stopped his buggy, and lifting his voice, said, "All the lights are out back there." He was shouting through the bows of the buggy top to Wilkins who was coming behind in another buggy, with Welt and the Welt woman. No light could be seen anywhere behind them. They could make out nothing except the blacker outlines of the tall Snyder barn just dimly relieved against a hint of the low prairie sky.

When, an hour later, Len Ormsbee and his wife were getting ready for bed, amid broken, half-whispered conjectures and fears, the woman rushed to the window of their bedroom, and her husband followed her. Some miles away a huge red blaze was climbing into the black sky. "Len, is it…is it…"

"Yes, it's the Snyder place. That's where it is… I…and I think it's the house…yes, it is, it's the house. I can see plain it's the house."

By the time the elder of the Welts and a few other men had arrived, after tying their horses far enough away to keep them from becoming too frightened by the fire, the roof was entirely gone and the walls were crumbling.

"Lucky there's no wind," one of the men said, "them sparks'd go clean to the barn if there was any breeze blowing in that direction."

"I'm not lookin' for sparks," Welt said, rather curtly.

Len Ormsbee came through the front gate, hurrying toward the little group of men standing on the lawn, and a woman came, running stumblingly, grabbing her skirts, behind him. "Where's Snyder?" he asked, looking intently into Welt's face. The latter shook his head, almost helplessly. "Well, we'd better be lookin' around for him then. In the orchard out there, and around them sheds back there behind."

The men moved off, going in a wide circle to escape the great heat of the fire. When they returned, a quarter of an hour later, coming one by one from out of the red glow that now permeated the orchard, they spoke to each other in short, quiet sentences, looking strangely into each other's faces. "Wasn't anybody back in the orchard. . . .Wasn't anyone at the barn... Ain't nothing around the sheds..."

A loud crash came out of the fire, and one of the upper walls tumbled downward amid fresh bursts of flame and puffs of swirling smoke. The smoke quickly disappeared, and a new brightness slowly spread through the blazing building. Something dark moved, as if alive, in the center of the fire. But it was indistinct, and might have been a tottering beam or steading. In a moment it appeared again, then fell headlong into the flames. "Did you see it?" asked the Welt woman, whispering hoarsely over a tall shoulder into her husband's ear. "Yes, I seen it. But don't you be scared that-a-way. It wasn't nothin', maybe. Just a timber, I guess."

The fire grew still brighter, less red and less smoky, and its bowels could now and then be seen twisting and writhing among the flames. More walls fell. The heat became greater, and the group on the lawn, increased now by other neighbors, moved farther from the burning house. "I think we'd better look around again," Ormsby said to the men. "Might be well to look closer in them sheds out there at the back of the house."

The men were even more silent and subdued than before, when they came back, some time later, from the direction of the orchard and the sheds. Some only shook their heads, to indicate that they had found nothing. The little group on the lawn, driven by the heat, had moved out to the road. One or two of the women were crying quietly. Two others started to go hurriedly away, looking backward over shawls that flapped at their shoulders. Another wall, the last left standing, leaned crazily, then crumbled into the fire. A flock of sparks arose and disappeared like tiny bright birds into the orchard.

But it was not long after this before the highest flames began visibly to subside. Soon a half-charred timber could be seen, jutting out of the glowing outer edges of the fire, like a large bone protruding from a quivering, mutilated body.

The fire continued to drop down and down, dying slowly with fitful bursts of flame. Some of the men began to go away. At last, after an hour or so, only a few remained. Ormsbee and Bert Wilkins told their wives to go on home without them. They would stay till morning.

Just before daylight the fire died into a wide pile of faintly glowing coals, and by sunup these were only a heap of ashes, above which wreaths of heat waves were constantly hovering. But because of the residual heat it was after noon before the men were able to rake the ashes apart with long-handled pitch forks. One of the men found some charred jewelry, a ring, a hat-pin, a badly molten brooch, another found two or three small coins in one place, and at another spot there was discovered what might have been the barrel of a gun. Nothing else of any significance was found. And as the men went away in small groups over the lawn scarcely anyone talked. A little while later half a dozen buggies moved off down the road, each with two or three farmers in it. A breath of moving air came out of the west and blew cool against the backs of their hands, where they could still feel the prick of the heat and the ashes. Suddenly the breeze died away, and the dull red light seemed everywhere to be glowing in the very air of the still May evening, falling upon the fences, the buggy tops, the flanks of the horses that were pulling the buggies, and the hats and faces of the silent men riding along the road.

6.

CUTTING DOCK

Tam Ryan was standing on the back steps of his little white house, his small reddish face tilted sidewise in an easy frown, his narrowed eyes blinking at the wet sunlit orchard. But Tam was not really looking at the orchard. He was gazing farther away, at a level black field already checkered with the faint green lines of young corn. He reached a groping hand up along the door jamb and stood leaning against his arm, one leg tossed carelessly across the other.

And now he heard his own voice speaking deep within him. It seemed to come out of him very deliberately and insistently. He could hear it telling him that there was no use thinking about plowing any more corn for a while. Not for a day or two, anyway. Maybe not for a week. Like all the heavens dropping sudden into the earth. It would be a good long time before a sensible man would be thinking of getting back into the field after that. It would be a good week, anyway.

Tam's frown became more thoughtful and serious. He looked more intently at the field out beyond the orchard. The rain coming in early June like this, just the right time for the corn. If it'd just stay warm now. Make the corn jump right up out of the ground. You'd just see it grow under your eyes, that's what you would. Come out like a man's Monday beard.

Tam's frown disappeared for a moment. A quick grin pushed the mobile corners of his mouth out into his reddish face. Then, suddenly, the frown had returned. Tam's eyes all but blazed with anger as they were fixed on the orchard. He had been cutting the dock in that orchard for the past twenty years. Every rainy day in the summer, he'd been down there with a scythe, sweating, and cursing the place. It wasn't anything for a grown man to be doing. You'd never get done with it. You might as well be trying to cut the devil's tail off. You could be working at it till the Judgment and you'd never get rid of it. Growing again, right after you, before you put the scythe away.

Tam's face changed again, slowly. He looked very grave, and perplexed. But you couldn't let all that burdock be growing up like that—not all of it anyway, the whole summer long. Especially on rainy days like this. Neighbors going past and looking in like they did. Always trying to see everything. Just like they didn't know all the other things a man had to do around a place.

Tam was looking now helplessly toward the orchard, his eyes wide and his reddish brows arched and complaining. Slowly and reluctantly he uncrossed his legs. He would go out and start on it, anyway. That's what he would do. He could cut for a little while. Maybe Milt Bowyer would come along, or one of the Corey boys. If they did, he might go on into town with them. He'd ought to go to town and see about things. Find out how the markets were going. Hadn't been down to town for he didn't know when. Seemed like months. Not since before he started plowing.

One of Tam's feet dropped heavily down from the step where he had been standing. His short legs carried him away from the house. He went down across the farm lot very slowly, his eyes dropped low as if to see whether his toes would keep moving in front of him.

After some time he came out from a low tool shed with a large scythe swaying awkwardly upon his shoulder. As he came back through the farm lot, he stopped once or twice to set the scythe handle on the ground and reach out to feel the blade. He shook his head contentedly, mumbling to himself. There was no need of putting the blade on the grinder. Just give it a good whetting. He'd have to ask the woman to turn the wheel if he put it on the grinder. When she was baking this way she'd be more fuss than help. As he went on past the house, he caught the sweet, dry smell of the baking. He held his eyes resolutely in front of him, as if refusing to look toward the kitchen.

Tam finally stopped in the thick shade of the pear tree down behind the chicken house. The dock was lighter there. He would just work into it sort of gradually. The sharp whang of the whetstone changed gradually to a shrill singing above his head. He let the scythe down slowly, then stood waiting for a while. His face turned and he gazed intently up the road. No one was coming. There was no sound of wagon wheels. As he turned back, he stared grimly down at the dock. Finally he spread his short legs and bent, almost angrily, over the scythe.

As the blade slid easily through the wet dock, Tam's twisted frown began to drift out of his face. Occasionally his eyes dropped for an instant to his swinging arms. He began to think of his mowing. He always could mow well. Not like some men he'd seen. Pulling things up by the roots. Digging into the ground like they thought they were ditching. Didn't mind mowing so much. Not after he got started. Tam felt the large damp green leaves dropping over his feet, as he pushed forward, step by step. He heard the smooth slicing sound of the blade as it went through the dock. He felt the slight pull and lift of the scythe in his arms and shoulders, the freer, easier rhythm of the mowing.

At last a dark wet finger or two began to spread out from the galluses on Tam's swaying back. Then he felt his shirt catching and pulling on his shoulders. Soon the scythe began to swing more slowly, leaving a narrower swath of the silvery green undersides of the great leaves behind it. Then the mowing had stopped entirely.

Tam lifted the scythe blade slowly. He reached up and grasped the blade, as if he were going to give it a further whetting. But he only stood there, leaning idly against the support of the scythe.

Out beyond the shade of the orchard, he saw the black field and the faint green lines of the corn. Farther away, the darker green of an oats field waved slowly out over a low hill. Beyond, but not very far away, masses of black and purplish cloud were dissolving in the white morning sun. Tam's eyes came back to the cornfield. Everywhere over the field the sun was pouring its thick warm light into the dark earth. Here and there long narrow strips, of glinting water lay between the rows of corn. Tam's gaze followed two of the faint green lines all the way across the field. His eyes were wide and bright now, and seemed filled with a quiet wonderment. He was thinking about the corn. How the rain would come like yesterday, and then the sun like it was this morning. And the corn would leap right up to your knees. And then up to your waist, and right up to your shoulders. Then the tassels would be there all at once, over the whole field. And the ears would come, on all the stalks. It was funny the way the corn grew up like that. Just from the seed you put down in the soft plowed ground.

Once in a while the shadow of a cloud pushed slowly across the field. Then the sun would return, brighter than before, pouring its warm light everywhere over the dark wet field. A kind of misty steam was now rising here and there, making the sunlight soft and almost creamy farther away, over at the other side of the field.

Then Tam again felt the dampness of his shirt. His face and hands seemed suddenly sticky. The air in the orchard had become very heavy, and it was filled with the prickling smell of the cut burdock. Tam's eyes dropped before him, in a sour stare at the uncut dock. He'd ought to get some more of it cut before it got any hotter. Slowly, reluctantly, he pulled the broken piece of whetstone from his back pocket, and now the still orchard rang for a few moments with an angry clanging. The scythe was dropped carelessly down among the burdock. Before starting to mow, Tam turned his head. His eyes followed the road to where, far away, it seemed to bend around the dark green blot of Jameson's orchard. No one was coming. He listened for some time. He couldn't even hear the remote clacking of wagon wheels.

Tam turned back and bent over the scythe again. His eyes began following the blade as it went back and forth among the thick stems of the dock. His face was very red now, and it was becoming wet and shiny. His arms kept swinging in a half circle before him, mechanically, listlessly. He went on working for a long time, his eyes glowering constantly down at the dock.

Suddenly the mowing stopped again. Tam stood tautly, his body still bent over the scythe. He turned his head quickly, and saw Milt Bowyer stopping his wagon out beside the orchard. Tam yanked the scythe out of the burdock. He tossed it lightly over his shoulder and started for the house, at the same time shouting to Bowyer to wait for a minute or two there on the road.

Tam stopped at the house, and poked his head in the kitchen door, the blade of the scythe sticking rakishly out behind him. "I'm thinking I'll have to be going in to town," he said, almost shouting. He raised his voice more confidently, till it went bawling through the house. "I'll have to be going down to the elevator to see about the markets now."

A large red-faced woman was bent over the stove in the kitchen, holding the door of the oven half-open while she examined the bread that was baking. Tam's voice suddenly dropped to a nervous complaining tone. "Milt Bowyer is going in to town in his wagon, and I'll just be going along and see about the markets."

The big woman shut the oven door and rose from the stove. She looked out at Tam, saying nothing.

"I'll just be leaving the scythe out here against the tree," Tam said, pleadingly. "You won't need to be bothering about putting it away. I'll be finishin' the dock this afternoon. I'll be back early."

The woman continued looking steadily out at Tam. Her big face was set queerly in a kind of contradiction. Her mouth seemed to be smiling and her eyes were filled with a kind of dull anger. "Tomorrow!" she said, her voice coming in a single, muffled snort.

Tam moved a step or two back from the door. He stood there,

hesitating for a few moments. Then he turned slowly, and with cautious steps went toward the big willow tree over beside the milk house. He leaned the scythe, blade uppermost, against the trunk of the tree. He started immediately toward the road. As soon as he had passed the house, he broke into a kind of loping half-run down through the tall uncut grass of the lawn. Then he went hopping back the road toward the wagon. His short legs scrambled over the big wheel, and at last he was perched on the high spring-seat beside Milt Bowyer. As the team started, he burst into a running torrent of talk, about everything—about the rain, about the corn, about his having most of the dock cut already, and his needing to go down to see about some things in town and find out what the markets were doing.

Just as they were passing the end of the orchard Tam glanced back over Bowyer's shoulder. He could just see his wife through the trees. She was standing out at the corner of the kitchen, her hand on her hip. Tam's face jerked back toward the team, and he burst out talking again, more rapidly and earnestly than before. After a little while his head again turned nervously and he looked back at the house. He could still see the big woman. Suddenly she went from the kitchen over toward the willow tree. He saw her grasp the scythe, then go down past the milk-house toward the tool shed. Tam began talking again, more emphatically than before, explaining to the silent man beside him about the rain yesterday, and how the corn would all be leaping right up out of the ground. Tam's face grew less nervous and more relaxed, but his voice ran on endlessly about the corn, at times rising to a kind of reckless, confident oratory. Why, that corn—nothing could hold it now. It would beat a Monday beard. It would be trying to jump away from its own roots. Grow like the devil's nails, that's what it would.

7.

NEWFANGLED MACHINERY

He had just finished the wheat cutting, and was pulling the binder in from the field. His body seemed as still and sharp as a scarecrow as he rode on through the red glow of the evening. Beside him the thin slats of the reel trembled and flashed in the intense light. Beneath him was the constant mad clanking and jangling of the binder.

The team turned wearily into the farmlot, and came to a stop over beside a low sagging shed, open at both ends, that leaned against a small gray barn. The man's legs were flung carelessly out from the binder. He dropped stiffly to the ground. His tall spare body turned slowly toward the light.

The man's arm now lifted idly and his hand grasped the seat above his head. The little hairs on the back of his hand became golden nettles in the slanting light. His long dark figure seemed to be hanging limp and motionless beneath the binder seat.

The man's face had become very quiet. The mouth dropped slowly open, like a dark rent in the yellow satin of his beard. He kept gazing out at the reddening prairies with eyes half-hidden in the purplish shadow of his wide straw hat.

He was watching two men who looked strangely small where they worked, far away, among numberless shocks of wheat. Beyond the men, the low hills dipped from their glowing ridges into widening blueish shadows. Above the hills, the sky was one vast motionless flame. The man beside the binder watched the men stooping and rising among the shocks, only half conscious that he was waiting for them to finish their work.

At last the man's gaze returned from the men and the hills to fall upon a nearer cornfield. He saw the narrow lane that ran down past the corn and on into the wheat field. All along the lane the corn stood like a high even wall, the great dark-green blades flashing continually in the brilliant light. Everywhere over the field the somber green of the corn was touched by a level, suspended sheet of fire. As he continued to gaze over the field, the fixed droop of the man's bearded lips lifted as though his face were about to break into an eager smile.

Suddenly the head was raised slightly. The wide brim of the hat tipped upward and the purple shadow flitted away from the man's squinted eyes. His face looked startled. He was gazing more intently into the glowing light. A persistent throbbing and humming seemed to come out of the very light itself. In a few moments a small dark object was moving along the red crest of one of the hills. Like a tiny bug, a tractor and binder crawled across the wide arch of western sky. A hint of golden dust accompanied it. A few moments later it slipped out of the light again, below the ridge of the hill. But the faint throb continued, droning steadily over the prairie like a sound dropping down from the sky.

The man's face had become fixed into a single twist of pain. The lips had straightened until they were hidden in his beard. The droning and throbbing went steadily on at times falling to a thin whine, then rising till it became a vibrant drumming in the air. Suddenly the beard quivered about the man's mouth. Then the lips moved. There was a quick splutter of words. The man seemed to be muttering something about machinery..."Cuttin' wheat with newfangled machinery...all of them like that now...gittin' smart and up-to-date...all their newfangled machinery."

Something haggard and painful crept into the old man's face for a moment. Then the dull eyes blazed again. "And all of them laughing that way...laughing and talking the way I heard...saying all those things about me...saying I'm gettin' old and queer..."

Instantly the man's face seemed to grow haggard again, and fearful. A moment later he broke into a kind of strangled laughter. "But I'm done...and they ain't...no they ain't...they ain't done cuttin'... they ain't."

His face was pushed far forward now, and the bearded jaw was jerking violently. He seemed to be laughing crazily up at the sky.

Finally the laughter stopped. The old man's gaze was fixed upon the hills. The droning and throbbing still came. But it was much fainter now. At last it seemed to stop. Then no sound drifted back from the hills and sky. Everywhere the glowing light seemed to be filled with a kind of dead and final silence.

There was a sudden rattle of harness chains, out where the horses stood in front of the binder. Then an iron wheel clanked, once, twice. The binder had moved a few feet, jerked forward by the restless team. As his hand dropped from the seat where it had been resting, the man turned to look down at the binder with a kind of petulant surprise. Then his gaze returned to the hills and the sky.

The flame was dulling and reddening along all the hills. The very crests of the hills had become charred and black. Lower, the wide blue shadows dipped into the darker swales. A duller, redder fight poured everywhere over the prairie.

The tall figure of the man was bent slightly forward. One of his hands jerked idly at a button on his greasy shirt. His face had become very quiet. Only his eyes were bright and wide with a strange excitement. His mouth had fallen loosely open. In the red fight a long snag of tooth glistened amidst his beard.

The voice came suddenly, as though rising out of his own mind. Then it was clearer, farther away. The man heard someone laughing now. Then he saw Jonas Hurst. Jonas was standing out beside the horses. And Pete was there too, standing behind Jonas, staring over Jonas' shoulder. Jonas was grinning crazily out of his small crooked face.

Now he could understand the words as Jonas spoke again. "What you doin'?" Jonas was still grinning as his high thin voice came clinking across the silence.

"You been dreamin' agin, that's what you been doin'." It was Pete who answered the question. The man saw Pete's mouth opening and shutting mechanically, his long dead face breaking into a pinched grin. The two men laughed abruptly, out beside the horses. Pete's laughter sounded like a sudden cackling.

Jonas was coming around the edge of the binder now. He looked intently up at the tall man who still seemed surprised, almost bewildered. "Well, I don't blame ye," Jonas said, his crooked face tilted upward till the rim of his hat nearly touched one of his shoulders. He kept punctuating his words with his quick tinkling laughter. "I don't blame ye at all. Got her all done, got her all shocked, every last bundle. Me and Pete. Got her all done."

Pete had stepped over among the horses' tugs now. He began unhitching. "Now you boys don't need to do that." The tall man had stepped impulsively toward the team. His voice was nervous, hesitant. "I can unhitch. I'll put the team up and feed them. You boys can go up to supper now. I'll put the team up. I just been waiting here. Not noticing the time."

The voice dropped timidly, then died away. The other two men laughed abruptly, as before. They were both busy among the tugs. A minute later the horses were trailing off toward the wooden water tank over beside the barn. Then they tramped wearily around to the barn door, their wet skin gleaming in the dull red light, pink dust spurting out from their big hoofs. A little while later the jangling of harness chains came from the barn. There was a swishing of hay, then the thud and grind of corn in the horses' feed boxes.

The three men stepped out of the barn and moved away toward

a low shanty standing beneath a windmill on a little rise. The figures of the three men became dark and sharp as they went swaying and bobbing into the red light. Their enormous shadows followed them across the farmlot. For a long moment they became very black against the sky, then were swallowed by the sharp edges of the shanty.

The sky had now become the color of coals seen through thin ashes. The light kept dropping slowly into the black crater of the hills.

8.

MASTER AND SERVANT

Zachary Morse had worked for J. B. Reynolds for fifteen years up to the past June, had planted J. B.'s corn with a famously straight "check," had stacked his hay, had milked his cows, broken his colts, shucked his corn (or always a good share of it), and had run the engine for Reynolds's threshing outfit—all apparently with an equable mind and certainly with all the dependability that J.B. ever asked of a man.

But now, on this rainy night of mid-August, when J. B. Reynolds's threshing was only half finished and the oats beginning to sprout in the shocks, on this rainy night Old Zachary was dead. He had died two days ago at dawn—just as the rainy spell was starting, almost at the hour at which always before he had gone out to his engine to get up steam for the day's threshing. He had "complained a little" all through the harvest season—from the very beginning of the oats-cutting; but he thought the pains that came were rheumatic merely—it had been such a wet summer. And lately he had clung to his engine seat only out of a stubborn tenacity of his will and the force of long habit—positively sick on some days, unwilling to stop working.

"Why, what you goin' to do?" he would ask in a high, irritated tone, whenever anyone would suggest his stopping work. "What'd J.B. do? He's got to get these oats out before the weather turns. Got to do it, and he's got to have somebody at the engine. Anyways, I'll be all right directly, I guess."

He would cling to his hard engine seat through the long hours of the day, with his eyes fixed upon the red throat of the separator which kept swallowing and swallowing the sheaves. Occasionally he would stoop down to the coal-wagon and pitch a few shovelfuls of fuel into the firebox. He scarcely said anything to anyone, but sat with his jaws set, his teeth biting his pipe constantly with the pain which he felt.

He never went to a doctor. He said he was all right, whenever anyone suggested it. And so he had died, quietly, but in greater pain than usual, only two days ago, before the doctor arrived—for J.B. had sent for the doctor at last without Old Zachary knowing it. J.B. was the only person in the world who could have prevented Zachary's working when sick, or who could have persuaded him to see a doctor. But J.B., following his own ways with men, had done neither; nor did anyone blame him exactly, now that Zach was gone. Heavy, sombre men came and sat a while in the kitchen—few of them went in to see Zachary in his plain coffin in the sitting room—but none of them thought of blaming J.B., as they called him. They understood: J.B. just didn't feel like doing a thing like that, like suggesting that Zach stop working, or go to a doctor. J.B. and old Zach had been so closely bound together that they always hid their intimacy, especially from each other; it was so strong and personal with them that they were ashamed to let it have any sort of expression. J.B. would have just felt awkward telling Zach to stop working or to go to a doctor; that was all. And so J.B. let the thing slide on, till Zach died at last, and nobody knew exactly what he had died from. And tonight while the rain kept falling in the oats field, J.B. sat in his kitchen with a few of his neighbors, hiding as well as he could the strange feeling which had crept over him since Zachary's death—a feeling of loss, as if he had been deprived of one of his limbs. At first he had felt pretty bad about it all, sad and rather shocked when the hard realization fully came to him that Old Zachary had really left him. But as he sat here this evening with his neighbors, who smoked their pipes so comfortably and talked about indifferent things, he was something like his everyday self again—the complacent, prosperous, almost genial J.B. He had been talking with his companions—mostly of the discouraging weather—when at last he reached over, knocked the ashes from his pipe into the coal bucket, and called for his wife in an unusually cheerful, hearty manner.

"Jennie!" He intoned the word, so that his voice lingered in the rooms of the house for some moments. "Jennie!"—and a little woman came to the kitchen door, with her hands folded in a large clean apron. "Jennie, would you get them cigars? Reckon you all like a cigar?" he said, turning to the men.

(J. B. Reynolds had bought cigars by the box only a few times in his life—only on such extraordinary family occasions as marriages or deaths or events of the most grave importance. And this was one of the decencies he would not have omitted for Old Zachary.)

There was an awkward minute or two, in the face of such unexpected hospitality. All the men lit and smoked their cigars uneasily, self-consciously—all except J.B. He liked a cigar greatly, though he did not smoke one often—"just never got into the way of it," as he would have said. And he smoked his cigar tonight with extreme satisfaction, experiencing a mild exultation in his own generosity, watching the others smoke, and not feeling the need to say anything, but only to toss clouds of tobacco smoke toward the kitchen ceiling. The others tried to make conversation, very unsuccessfully, with short halting comments. Then a little man named McCray, who sat almost in the door, who had not yet succeeded in saying anything, and who felt particularly awkward, said abruptly, "Well, guess Zach would like this all right. Always did like a good smoke."

This made matters only more sharply awkward; for most of the farmers had studiously avoided the dead man as they had talked on during the evening. A number of cigars glowed intensely, as if to burn away the difficulty with hard smoking. But J.B. only smoked on as usual. The remark had not disturbed his composure at all. And he said, very quietly, "Yes, Old Zach would like it—that's what he would." And then he nodded thoughtfully to himself several times. "Good Old Zach—always did like his smokin'."

This was confirmed by half a dozen solemn voices, one after another. "Didn't care f'r cigars, though," J.B. went on to say. "Always wanted his old pipe. Remember, he never smoked a cigar 'cept once to my knowledge."

Then J.B. began to smile shrewdly but kindly, and he glanced at one or two of the other men. "That was the time he was goin' to get married," he said.

A smile came over each solemn face in the kitchen. Old J.B. looked up at all of them, and his smile was broader and kindlier. Then his chair came down from its tilt, and J.B.'s elbows rested on his knees, while he looked through the grating into a dull fire in the stove.

The smile suddenly vanished again, and was gone for a few moments. "Poor Old Zach," he said, and then smiled again.

J.B. discovered that his cigar was nearly out. He pulled at it for a half-minute with great concentration. Then he leaned back in his chair again and noted the glowing end of his half-cigar with satisfaction. No one said anything, and everyone knew that J.B. was going to tell something—some favorite reminiscence of Old Zach. All the reluctant fear about disclosing his fondness for the man who had served him so long now seemed to be dropping from J.B. under the spell of the cigars.

"You remember when Old Zach was goin' to get married," he said, flicking some ashes compactly half-way to the coal bucket where they scattered with a splashing effect upon the linoleum.

"You all remember when he went away that time, don't you?" he said.

Everybody remembered it, but none, of the men in the kitchen were smiling about it now. They didn't know what J.B. was going to make out of the matter, and they were all waiting for their cue. You always had to let J.B. come to the point in his own fashion, in his own good time—but tonight nobody much minded if the point had to wait till the end of his cigar.

"Remember how he explained it when he came back?" J.B. went on, abruptly looking up at all his listeners and chuckling a little. "Yeah, he said she wouldn't come out and live in the country. He said she wouldn't leave the city—she wanted to be a town gal, as Zach put it. He said she objected, when it come down to it, to comin' out to the country. I remember yet just how he ended up the story. 'Yep,' he said, 'I just turned her down right then and there. She'd either come out with me and live with me out here, where I could be aworkin' on a farm like I always have been, or else I didn't want her. No city dolls fer me,' he said. And that was all Zach ever said about it. From that day on he never mentioned the affair once."

The cigar smoke went up in bluish clouds here and there over the kitchen. After a minute or so somebody said something about a "light," and a match was taken from the big box on top of the stove. J.B. remained leaning backward at his sharp angle, and was silent for a while, only blowing one cloud of tobacco smoke after another into the heavy air. A strange shrewd smile kept playing about his eyes, and there was an immense curious satisfaction in his face.

"Of course that was just Zach's own story, you know," was the way in which J.B. continued his talk.

"You don't think he was goin' to get married at all then, when he went away?" asked big Arch Timmons from the other side of the kitchen stove.

"No, don't at all," answered J.B.

"Course, his not even sayin' anything about it afterward was strange," admitted little McCray over in the corner by the door.

"Yeah, that's one reason," said J.B. with a wrinkle of frown above his eyes. "But I just sort of felt all along there never was anything to it. Fact, I hadn't any doubt about it at all. Never believed Zach thought of gettin' married."

"Well, why do you suppose he said it?" asked little McCray, at the edge of his chair with curiosity.

"Well, you know Zach had seen lots of the world afore he came out to work f'r me on that June day fifteen years ago. And you know he never went nowheres much after he came. Stayed right with me. Best hand I ever had—and I'll say it now, he was the best hand I ever expect to have." Well, that time he went away—in the last of May it was—yes, it was just six years ago—he had been with me then f'r nine years. Well, I think that all at once he just took one of his old natural notions to move—and it just got the best of him. Till he just decided he'd have to go. And it had been botherin' him f'r some time, as I could see. He wrote some letters and got one from somebody—I don't know who or how. And then he told me he was goin'. But poor Old Zach—when it came down to it he couldn't hardly do it. And when I asked him why, he was all but lost. He didn't know what to say. Seemed as if he couldn't think of anything. He stammered around awhile, and then finally that's what he told me. 'Fact is, boss,' he said, 'I'm goin' to get married.' And he smiled sheepish-like and looked down at the ground, and I never did see anybody look so queer as Zach did then. But that was Zach for you. He just went to pieces whenever he knew he was in the wrong—he was just made that way, that was all. That was on Friday he told me, I remember, and he said he was goin' next day—Saturday, and the weddin' would be Saturday night in the city. He asked if he could have the rig to drive over to the village that evening to get shaved and to get a few clothes. I told him yes. And so he went. I was still sittin' up when he came home from the village. Was sittin' on the porch when he came in. Course he stopped and seemed to be lookin' f'r me. Reached in his pocket and took out a couple cigars. Gave me one. And we both sat and smoked f'r a while. Joked a little about the weddin', for Zach was a little cooler now. Had sort o' got control of himself.

"Well, anyway, he went off the next day. I didn't say much. He drew up all his wages. And I thought then there was something in the wind more than a weddin'. Took him to the train—and I tell you he shook hands rather sheepish too. Yes, sir. Course I hated like everything to see him go. Never hated to see any man leave so much before. But off he went. And I just had to smile a little when it was all over, as I drove home by myself.

"Then of course you know the rest—how he turned up again. Just about two weeks later. Said he'd decided not to get married after all. Said the girl wouldn't leave the city, that she wanted to be a city gal, a city doll I think it was he called her. Said he was back to work f'r me now f'r good.

"And, and—I don't mind sayin' now that I was mighty glad to see him back too. But, by George, I don't think I was half as glad as he was to get back—no, sir. Just like a dog comin' home after bein' lost—just like that. Glad as everything to be with me. I could see it."

And J.B. leaned back in his chair still farther than before, and hooked the thumb of his cigar hand into a pocket of the old vest he was wearing, and smoked with the old pleasure of the master who remembers that one man has served him for the sheer joy of doing so.

Then the butt of his cigar began to grow hot in his fingers. He took a few more draughts of the smoke deep into his lungs, then tossed the stub into the stove after opening one of the small round lids.

Someone was rising, as if making to go home. "Oh, won't you have another cigar, boys?" asked J.B., reaching for the box on top of the stove.

"No, no, thanks, J.B.," someone said, "the family will be waitin' f'r me and worryin' if I don't get along."

And one after another of the men arose from his chair, each putting his cigar stub into the stove as J.B. had done, and each offering some apology for leaving as he went out into the storm.

J.B. sat alone in the kitchen when all the neighbors were gone. The other members of his own family were going upstairs now. His wife came to the kitchen door and suggested that J.B. had better come to sleep also. No, he would better stay up, he guessed—someone ought to stay up, he thought. Then his wife went upstairs, one slow step after another, till at last all was still in the house except the dropping now and again of a heavy shoe above.

J.B. lit another cigar and slouched in his chair. Through the smoke as it circled about him he remembered again the dead man, and looked through the door now and again toward the plain black coffin in the sitting room where it was dimly lit by one small light which had been turned very low. J.B. then listened to the rain upon the window, and he wondered when they would ever get back to the threshing. And then he remembered Old Zach sitting on the threshing engine and suddenly forgot the rain again; and smoked steadily, thinking and thinking of Zachary Morse, and mixing with his strong honest affection just that filament of vanity which makes the master foolish where the servant was comparatively wise,—while the rain in the oats fields came down and down and there was no star for a candle, but only a dim coal-oil lamp burning through the night beside a plain black coffin in the other room.

9.

BALAAM IN BURRVILLE

Peter Slagg had decided to get mules. Horses were always getting sore shoulders or becoming wind broken or something. So just before the breaking for wheat began he went down into Missouri and came back with a span of big bay mules. They were just the thing, as tall and almost as heavy as horses, and as lithe and tough as hickory saplings.

One of the mules—Big Jim—was a great worker. But Old Belle was as lazy and shrewd as her birthplace could have made her. Peter saw, the very first day of plowing, that he would have to show her that he meant what he said whenever he shouted at her to "Gat out a there, fast—fast, I say, you low-down Missouri half-breed." But when Peter hit her with his long nasty whip—a hedge stick with thorns trimmed off, to which was attached a strap of tough leather with a lash of corded whang at the end—the mule would only hunch her back, kick stiffly with both heels at the singletree, and then move on as slowly as before. As Peter told some of his neighbors, she was about the orneriest thing he'd ever seen between a pair of tugs.

Of course everyone around Burrville immediately heard about Peter and the mules. The men spent all one Saturday evening laughing about it in the barber shop, and whenever they congregated down at the "grain office," Pete's mules were sure to be mentioned.

Everybody said it was just about the best thing they'd heard in a good while.

That is, everyone except Mrs. Jenny Tyle. The widow Tyle lived in a little white house up on Maple Street, and she was certainly one of the nicest people in Burrville. She was the only lady in town who belonged to the Humane Society over in Gibeon, the county seat—some folks even said she was a charter member. When she heard the news about Peter Slagg and the mules she was aghast, and went over to Bert Ronaldson's immediately to see if something couldn't be done about it. Bert was the local real estate dealer and insurance agent, and lived next door to Mrs. Tyle. When Bert said that he didn't see hardly how anything could be done about it and tried to explain that a mule could always stand hard work and whippings better than horses anyway, he was bluntly told that he was a brute for saying such things.

But it was only a few days later that Bert came into town one evening and told what he had seen at the Slagg place where he stopped for a minute as he was returning from over near Shilo where he had been looking at a piece of land. Bert had found Pete out in the field along the road, plowing with the mules. "Jist the contrariest thing I ever laid a whip to," Pete said, in answer to Bert's question. Pete was carrying a very curious looking whip—the usual hedge stick with the long leather strap attached, but with the whang lash now replaced by a short piece of new barbed wire. Bert saw that Pete didn't care to talk much. He looked tired, and his shirt was wet around his shoulders and down his back. As Bert drove off down the road he kept looking back through the buggy bows, and he saw Pete moving slowly up the field. Every once in a while he would whip the off mule. The mule would spurt into a half-trot for a rod or two, and then lapse into her habitual gait. But the hedge on the Semmes place soon blotted Pete from view, and Bert rode on toward town grinning to himself.

When Bert drove into the livery barn an hour or so later and told about Pete and the whip, the men sitting on the old chairs beside the office all laughed heartily. Kel Higgins, who worked around the barn, said it was just what you'd expect of Pete Slagg. But the Everyman himself, Jesse Hunter, when he had finally stopped scratching his head and grinning, declared it really beat all he'd ever heard. "Nope, never heard a usin' barbed wire even on balkers."

The news soon spread over town, and finally drifted up Maple Street. Mrs. Ronaldson casually told Mrs. Tyle about it over the back porch, as Bert was washing up for supper. The widow Tyle heard it in silence, with prayerful horror. Afterwards she wept quietly, sitting on the little blue chair in her kitchen. Then, taking off her white bib apron, she left the house and went practically the length of Maple Street in an effort to create moral indignation. Her hair, tucked loosely under the little black straw hat, shook furiously whenever she talked to people at open doors. She kept her thin hands clutched on her bosom, and her eyes blazed whenever she mentioned the name of "that Slagg man." And her pale, narrow face was almost tense and desperate as if she were organizing a lynching mob.

But what can a woman do to bring the light of a humane ideal into the darkened conscience of a town like Burrville? At almost every door, Mrs. Tyle's eloquence was met by little more than the rustling of newspapers in the hands of merchants waiting for their suppers. Some of the housewives listened politely, but most of them were plainly impatient to get back to their kitchens. Mrs. Davis even said she was afraid her meat was burning! And many of the children grinned—actually grinned while Mrs. Tyle talked. The brats of Burrville! What could be done with such children, who came, all of them, from such ungodly cradles?

Later in the evening Mrs. Tyle sat for a long time in her chill parlor, forgetting her supper, occasionally smothering little sighs and sobs with a wet handkerchief. When at last the dusk had deepened along Maple Street and it was almost dark in the parlor, she reached under the gilt fringe of the old blue-paper shade and lit the big oil lamp that sat on the table beside her. Then she gently lifted her Bible from the table, opened it tenderly, and began reading. "And Balaam arose in the morning, and saddling his ass, went with them.... And when Balaam beat her, and had a mind to bring her again in the way.... The ass said: Am I not thy beast, upon which thou hast been always accustomed to ride until this present day? Tell me, if I ever did the like thing to thee." Her reading finished, Mrs. Tyle sat for a long time in silence, holding her crumpled handkerchief in her lap. Then she left her chair, went in to the big wooden bed in her little low bedroom, and at last fell asleep. And that night, as certain people in Burrville have since said, Jennie Tyle dreamed that a great flood came up from Missouri, and that no man in all Burrville had an ark, and that the pitiful braying of many asses was mingled with the roaring of the waters. But of course this was only a story. Perhaps we shall never surely know whether she had such a dream or not.

But at any rate when the Burrville Tribune Gazette came out four days later there appeared on the first page an article entitled "Cruelty of Local Citizen." No names were mentioned, but much was said in the article about beasts that are better than their masters. The article was signed "Jane Priscilla Tyle."

As things happened, on the day before the Tribune Gazette appeared, Peter Slagg was finishing the sowing of his winter wheat. And Peter, two or three times a year, celebrated the conclusion of his greater seasonal labors by spending a few extra dollars in town. So on this day, which was a Saturday, he came to Burrville a little before noon, and in the evening went home singing. When he got home he found, awaiting him, his copy of the Tribune Gazette, which had come in the mail at noon. His slightly shining eye immediately caught "Cruelty of Local Citizen."

He read it from beginning to end, very soberly, sitting on the edge of his low porch. Then he began to laugh to himself, very quietly at first, but afterwards so loudly that the chickens standing about in the yard started to cackle excitedly.

When Pete's laughter subsided, a strange smile began to spread over his face, and his already shiny eyes suddenly became brighter still. Then he arose from the porch and went directly to the barn, where he fed his mules a heaping armload of corn, almost as much as he had given them during the whole of the previous week. After returning to the house he went off to bed early to a long and very sound sleep.

The next morning—which was Sunday, of course—he did not arise until almost noon. He took a hasty bachelor's breakfast of eggs and coffee, and followed this with some brandy from a bottle on the kitchen table. A little while later he put his copy of the Tribune Gazette very carefully into his rear trousers pocket and went off to the barn. Very deliberately and with an air of great seriousness, he led Old Belle from her stall, clambered onto her narrow back and rode slowly down the farmyard lane to the front gate, where he turned the mule toward Burrville.

Peter Slagg rode up the sabbath stillness of Maple Street about mid-afternoon with a gay, almost jaunty air, the old slouch hat tilted far back on his head. His hands lay, one upon the other, on the mule's withers. His eyes occasionally looked upward through the openings of the arching trees into the blue sky above Burrville. His legs dangled easily at the sides of the mule, the toes of his big shoes bobbing regularly up and down with every slow step of the animal. There was an abstraction from all the common things about him, a vast freedom of spirit in the whole aspect of Peter Slagg, suggesting perhaps some grand, quixotic purpose in his mind.

He stopped the mule in front of Mrs. Tyle's, and with the air of a man who is very sure of himself, looked at the little house standing back from the street amidst the cool shade of the maple trees. Then he turned the mule toward the curb, and rode across the sidewalk with a sharp clatter and on over the smooth green lawn, carefully avoiding a bed of asters, just as Solomon would have done.

At the corner of the porch he dismounted, and tied the mule to one of the white wooden columns. He took the copy of the Tribune Gazette from his pocket, unfolded it, and gently placed it, like a fly net, over the animal's rump. Backing a few paces over the lawn, he stood for a while gazing approvingly at the mule. Then he turned and stalked away, walking through the bed of asters around which he had so carefully guided the mule.

Old Belle gazed suspiciously about her until suddenly her ears stood up sharply. There was a stifled scream, then an intense silence during which the scream echoed far away up Maple Street. Jenny Tyle stood quivering in the doorway, her small white form dimly outlined behind the wire of the screen door. She was staring speechless at the mule. Suddenly she saw Pete disappearing below the horizon formed by the small of a mule's back. She tried to scream at him, but choked with increasing terror and anger, while Peter Slagg kept walking down Maple Street with an air of great dignity and composure.

The mule now began to pull steadily backward at the hitch rein, her haunches sinking lower and lower until the newspaper fell fluttering to the ground. Mrs. Tyle disappeared from the screen but soon came timidly out at the far end of the porch, through the dining room door. She began to call for help in a high, trembling voice. "Mister Ronaldson, Mister Ronn-aldson. Help me, oh help me, save me, Mister Ronaldson."

When Bert Ronaldson burst out on his porch, he stopped abruptly, staring in amazement at the mule, while he heard the widow Tyle begging him to protect her, to save her, to take the awful beast away. Then a slow, understanding grin spread over Bert's face as he went slowly down his front steps and moved over onto Mrs. Tyle's lawn.

By this time Ed Hutchinson, the cashier of the Farmers and Traders Bank, and Ben Saunders, who ran the Burrville grain house, appeared on the lawn. They moved over near where Bert was standing. "Walk right up to her, Bert," Ed said, in the same assuring manner in which he would advise a man to buy a new house or a piece of land, except for a slight quiver in his usual suave voice. "Don't let her think you're afraid of her." "Better slip up to her from the side," Ben

Saunders said excitedly. "I tell you, Bert, you're takin' chances if you don't. Better just edge up along the porch there, Bert. Get in to her kind a sidelin' like, you know." Bert went a little closer to the mule. "Whoooaa, now...whoa, whoa, mule," he said, taking another step nearer the beast. Suddenly the mule bared her large yellow teeth, and there was a slight fluttering in her flanks as she raised one of her small dainty hoofs a few inches from the ground.

As Bert backed quickly away there came a scream, and Mrs. Ronaldson ran out of a group of women that had gathered over on the Ronaldson lawn. She began pulling at the white sleeve of Bert's shirt, begging him to come away with her. When Bert quietly told her that he couldn't go with her, she quit pulling at the sleeve but began to cling to him tenaciously, hugging one of his arms with both her hands.

Up on the porch, Mrs. Tyle stood taut and motionless. All through the excitement she had been unable to say anything, but had clutched her hands frantically on her bosom. Between tense, gasping breaths, she now began begging Bert to leave the mule alone. "You will get killed, you will get killed… Oh! Mr. Ronaldson, don't get killed…"

Bert turned to Ed Hutchinson and Ben Saunders, and they talked quietly among themselves for a minute. Then Bert hurried over the grassy driveway toward his own house, with Mrs. Ronaldson following. A little while later he could be heard talking loudly over the telephone. "Irie...say Irie (Ira Bankson was the Burrville marshal). Get Pete Slagg if you can. He ought to be around town there somewheres. Bring him up to Mrs. Tyle's house, will you? And say, maybe you'd better bring Jesse Hunter along. Explain to you when you come up. Try and find him, will you?"

Just as Bert came out of his house, a little black and yellow dog bounded across the street and began to dodge and bark at the mule's heels. The mule turned her head and watched the dog intently. Suddenly her heels went upward...once, twice. The little dog dodged sidewise, then crept away toward the street, snarling a little as it went.

Mrs. Tyle's face had now turned the color of her muslin bosom, and she was wringing her hands until the ruffles at her wrists looked like a cloud of little white butterflies.

But sticks, rocks, and an occasional empty milk bottle had now begun to fly at the mule. Boys were shouting gleefully, and Ben Saunders was shouting angrily at the boys.

Then Lafe Timmons came striding across the lawn, shouting in his great booming voice that rose above all the rest of the noise. He was telling everyone to keep still. When the others had finally stopped shouting, Lafe turned to Bert Ronaldson and said, "You can't do anything with that mule this way, Bert. You're scarin' her with all this hollerin'. You're gettin' her all excited." Everyone listened attentively to Lafe. He was the Burrville butcher and was of course used to handling rather wild cattle. He was hatless, and even on a Sunday afternoon like this, he was wearing his blue working shirt and his big greasy overalls.

"I tell you, Bert," he said, "the only way you can handle 'at mule is t' get up t' her head. Got t' kind a come at her from the front, you see. Now Bert, you keep 'em quiet out here, and I'll see what I can do. Don't think she'll be much trouble if everybody just keeps quiet fer a while."

As Lafe was starting up the steps, he stopped and turned to Mrs. Tyle. "Now, Mrs. Tyle," he said, "you don't need to be scared. There ain't no danger. An' we're goin' to have this mule out a here in a jiffy." Lafe then went boldly up on the porch and then over to the column where the mule was tied. He reached confidently for the taut rein. Suddenly Old Belle's tail dropped low between her hind legs, and she bit savagely at Lafe's hand, missing it narrowly. Then she snapped at the hand again, this time catching Lafe's blue sleeve and pinching his forearm lightly but painfully. Lafe backed away from the mule, and went slowly down the steps, grasping his arm where he had been bitten, his face twitching slightly with the pain of it.

In the midst of the excitement that followed—a woman somewhere out near the street had now started to cry, and Mrs. Tyle had shrunk, quivering and almost hysterical, to the very farthest corner of the porch—Ira Bankson came straight across the lawn, his broad suspenders pale against his dark shirt, the star glittering on his breast. With him was Jesse Hunter, the livery-man. And between them walked Peter Slagg, owner of the mule.

Half way across the lawn they stopped, while Bert and Lafe hurried over to meet them, followed by Ed Hutchinson and Ben Saunders. After Bert had quietly explained things—with several loud interpretations from Lafe—Ira Bankson spoke curtly to Pete Slagg and then hooked his thumbs in his suspenders quizzically, while Jesse Hunter pushed Pete gently and encouragingly toward the mule.

As Peter Slagg came on over the lawn toward the porch, Mrs. Tyle watched him in terrified silence. She saw his long arms, his strong, brutal hands. Was he going to beat the defenceless mule? Would he kill the poor creature? The widow Tyle stood trembling, her white dress billowing over the porch rail, her whole body palpitating like that of some huge frightened hen.

Then suddenly Mrs. Tyle saw in the face of Peter Slagg something that made her little eyes widen incredulously.

There was positively a radiant benignity in the man's face. His eyes had become tender, like those of a mother pacifying an irritated chid. And when a gentle twitching came at last into the corners of his mouth, he began to speak, quietly and kindly, to the mule. "Nice Old Belle," he said. "Nice Belle...whooaa...steady now...nice Belle." The mule looked at Peter, and she seemed pleased, for she twitched her stumpy tail once or twice. A large, horny hand moved slowly upward and patted the mule's neck, and then reached for the hitch rein and untied it from the porch with a little jerk at the bow knot.

And Peter Slagg then did a gallant thing. He led the mule a few steps back from the porch, took off his green felt hat that was stained and caked at the band with the sweat of many summers of plowing and horse-whipping, and with a stiff but sweeping gesture, saluted the lady on the porch.

A few minutes later he rode away through the gathering dusk along Maple Street. Astride his mule, he went out of Burrville with a joyous, peaceful heart, and the last red glory of the prairie evening took Pete Slagg and the mule slowly to itself.

10.

WINTER WHEAT

Every night he sat before the base burner this way, staring into the coals. His ashen eyes were sunk deep behind broad shiny cheek bones, and his chin fell loosely down from his mouth onto his soiled gray shirt. His whole body was small, and seemed very old. The shoulders fell slightly outward from the back of a sagging wicker chair. Two long bony hands lay motionless on the stiff knees.

Sometimes the man would raise one of his hands quickly to choke back a sudden fit of coughing. But the coughing would become more and more violent, until at last the man's whole body was shaking and trembling. Gradually and very slowly, the coughing would subside. Afterward a livid redness would remain for some time in the sunken face.

Except for the occasional fits of coughing, there was practically no sound or movement in the house. A clock ticked somewhere behind a door. A coal-oil lamp kept spluttering and flaring in its high bracket above the man's head. The tiny blue flames played constantly over the red coals in the base burner.

Over on the other side of the stove sat a plain woman in a tall rocker, a long needle moving steadily in her strong capable hands. There was something dark and foreign in her face, which was very broad and square. Now and then the corners of her mouth moved nervously. Under the shadow of her heavy hair, her deep eyes were very soft and dark. Occasionally she peered anxiously across the room at the man in the wicker chair.

Back on a low couch in a shaded corner of the room sat a young man, erect and awkward. His smooth boyish face was strained out of the shadows toward the stove. He seemed anxious and somehow embarrassed as he stared over at the man sitting so motionless in the chair.

The house had become very still. There was only an occasional creak of a studding or rafter as the wind rose to a low moan in the trees outside. Once in a while a flutter of snow would brush the black window pane beneath the flaring oil lamp. Sometimes a few harder flakes would bite sharply against the glass. The cold tinkling sound would drop bitterly into the room.

The man began coughing again, suddenly and convulsively. The woman rose and went silently over to his chair. Her dark head and shoulders were bent far over him. Her hand supported his shaking head. The coughing continued for a long time, but at last gradually subsided with a series of prolonged wheezing sobs.

The woman went back to her chair. The needle flashed in her fingers again. She kept glancing anxiously past the stove toward the small figure in the low willow chair. After a while the woman suddenly asked, "Are you getting cold now? Hermann, I am talking to you. You are getting cold?" Her voice was rich and very quiet. The man merely shook his head. His bony face seemed utterly sunken and exhausted. There was a slight twitching in his gray lips. He was gazing petulantly, almost childishly, down into the fire.

Suddenly all the coals clinked loudly and shifted lower in the stove. The fire purred contentedly for a few moments. After that the house seemed more quiet than before. The clock was again ticking somewhere in another room. The snow no longer bit against the window, but came very softly like a steady whispering at the dark pane. There was hardly any moaning above the house now.

The man's gaze lifted from the stove. He looked across at the woman. Her knitting continued for some time, then stopped. The needle became a slit of light against her dark dress. She looked across at the man and noticed his eyes lifted toward her own. All the petulance seemed to have gone from his mouth now. A kind of strained gentleness had come into his face.

"Are you feeling better now?" the woman asked. "Hermann? You are better now?" The voice was more quiet than before.

The faint hint of a smile crossed the man's face. "Yes," he said in a kind of hoarse whisper.

The woman rose silently and went over to his chair again. Her dark head leaned over him as before. "You feel rested now? It must be nine o'clock, almost. You better go to bed."

The man's face was raised slightly, and a smile loosened the tight shiny skin below his cheeks. "Yes," he said, "I guess I better..." The whisper broke chokingly in his throat. Quick pain and a kind of childish terror came into his lifted eyes. He kept looking up at the woman this way for some time, his whole face tremulous and desperate. Gradually the pain and terror seemed to leave his eyes. At last he managed to say, "I guess I better... I... I'll go now." The whispered voice was now steady, but still thick and labored.

The boy had moved from the couch, and was standing across from his mother, at the other side of the chair. Together they bent down and lifted the man's spare form. As the woman turned to reach for the lamp, the man leaned forward upon the boy's arm. His short figure was stooped and worn, but he did not seem so thin or frail now. There was a hunched compactness in his back and shoulders, a stony hardness in his jaw and in his dangling hands. There were only an unnatural hollowness in his chest, and a shiny pallor in the sunken cheeks.

As the woman brought the lamp down from the wall, the flame spluttered frantically in the small globe. Then the three stood waiting silently for a little while. There was a sudden louder moaning outside, followed by a steadier fluttering of the snow over at the window. The man's face strained around toward the black pane. As he listened to the snow for a moment or two, a feeble smile trembled out of his shiny eyes: He looked up at the boy. "It'll be good for the wheat," he said with quick pain streaking through the faint smile on his face.

After that the three shuffled away from the fire, the man stooped and leaning upon the big woman and the slender figure of the boy. They went through the dark frame of a door over in the corner of the room. The dim yellow light moved across another room; for a moment it glinted against a picture hanging on a remote wall. Now bulging, grotesque shadows were pushing and swaying about the other room, and soft, indistinguishable sounds came as if from the shadows themselves.

After a little while the boy came back through the low frame of the door. He stood tall and dark against the red light of the stove, looking steadily down into the dance of blue flames among the coals. His reddened cheeks flowed smoothly out from the shaded pockets of his eyes.

At last the woman came back through the doorway, her broad face lighted brightly by the lamp in her hand. She looked at the boy anxiously as his eyes were raised questioningly to her face. The woman's heavy lips began to tremble. "He...was talking again," she said. "I had to come away. He....knows everything...just as well as we do... He was talking about you, and about the snow coming this way, and how green it will make the wheat in the spring.... He...he said how green the wheat will be for you in the spring.... He just kept talking that way... I... I had to come away..."

As the woman, and the boy went on staring into each other's faces, the coals again shifted in the stove with a louder clink, then purred quietly as before. After that the snow seemed to come more steadily over at the window.

11.

THE QUARREL

With a rusty tin full of coal oil in one hand and a clump of greasy rag in the other, he kicked at the screen door until it became dislodged from the jamb, and then edged his way out. The door slapped behind him and the released spring whirred for a moment or two as the old man shuffled away from the back porch, his face bent and frowning over the cup of coal oil that kept spilling upon his hand at almost every step.

He went over to the lawn in a kind of scurrying half run, passed through the dappled shade of the maple tree, then across the narrow dirt drive and on toward a clump of burdock in a corner of the small farmyard. He set the cup on the ground, then began tugging and jerking at the handles of a plow that was half hidden among the weeds. He stood for a moment frowning at the plow and muttered to himself. Then he bent over painfully and began splashing the rusty share with the oil.

Little specks of brightness appeared here and there on the share as Nate Heming rubbed at it steadily. But the old man's brow was moist now, and a filmy, misty blur was gathering just before the gray lashes of his eyes, so that he could hardly see the brightness coming on the share. Suddenly dropping the stub of corn cob with which he had been rubbing at the rust, he lifted his body painfully and stood for a while shaking his head at the share and grumbling unintelligibly to himself. He rubbed the back of a greasy hand across his eyes and the little bright spots on the share suddenly began winking up at him.

"I... I can't scour the thing," he said, "I won't scour it."

Suddenly his head jerked backward angrily. A dense flock of blackbirds was passing over the barn. They swooped downward into the pasture with a great whirring of wings. Their raucous chattering ceased abruptly.

"Now look at that," the old man almost shouted, his shrunken face growing taut with the lines of violent anger. "I'll tell you, I'm goin' to put an end to that."

He hurried away to the house, then in a little while returned, holding a single barrelled shotgun crosswise before him. He stole around the corner of the barn, and a minute later the sound of a shot came from the pasture. A harsh din arose as the birds, lifting in a black cloud, went off northward over the fields in swift, trailing flight. Then Nate Heming came back from the pasture, tramping heavily through the farmlot, the gun over his shoulder, his face flushed but relieved.

He was half way to the house when a woman burst out of the screen door on the rear porch and came toward him with long, rapid strides.

"Now what are you doin'? Don't try to fool me, Nate Heming. I heard you shootin' out there." The woman had planted her large body directly in front of Nate and her great jaws worked heavily while she talked.

Nate looked at the woman but said nothing.

"What you doin' with that gun, I said."

"Been shootin' blackbirds. That's what I been doin', ef you want to know so bad."

"Give me that gun."

The woman snatched the gun out of Nate's hands, then pointed a brown arm toward the half scoured plow over beside the fence.

"Now you git over at that plow, Nate Heming. Just like I told you this morning... You ought to been in that tater field an hour ago. Lord knows, you've had enough time to git a dozen plows scoured."

Nate put one hand in his pocket, turned casually and started toward the plow. The woman stood watching while he moved away, her face squinted into a fixed, dry smile.

Half way to the plow the old man turned abruptly about, shook his fist violently at the woman and shouted, "I tell you, Sadie Heming, you ain't goin' to give me no dog's life this way. I... I'm not goin' to be worked to death. You just don't know what you're doin', you don't. You're just drivin' me right to my grave, that's what you're doin', Sadie Heming." The old man turned toward the plow again as he spoke of going to his grave, and his voice grew suddenly low and husky.

The big woman turned and went slowly toward the house, carrying the gun awkwardly at her side. But as she was crossing the dirt drive between farm lot and the lawn she stopped and looked back. Nate was standing beside the plow, a corn cob in his hand, glaring at her. A grimace of disgust spread over Sadie Heming's face.

"Er you goin' to plow that tater field this afternoon or not?" she asked, lifting her voice to suit the distance.

Nate flung the corn cob into the burdock beside the fence, "No," he said abruptly. Then he spoke slowly and deliberately. "I guess I don't plow that tater field."

Mrs. Nate Heming went over to the maple tree and leaned the gun against it, then returned rapidly across the farm lot.

She stooped and picked up the can of coal oil and a corn cob, then rose and stood facing Nate, her mouth drawn tight over her teeth and her eyes flashing. "All right," she said in a low but unsteady voice. "You don't need to. I'm goin' to scour this plow, Nate Heming, and I'm goin' to plow that tater field. You don't need to."

Nate gulped audibly before he said, "Just you go ahead and try it. Just go right on an' try it, old woman." A thin smile pulled at the corners of his mouth and his whole body trembled slightly as he burst, first into a low, wheezy chuckle, then into a dry laugh. "I jess sees you a-plowin' that tater field. You'll learn, you'll learn what kind of work I have to do around here... An' it won't be like fussin' inside a house all day, neither."

Mrs. Sadie Heming jerked her head back and looked straight into Nate's flashing eyes as she said, "Yes, an' I'll tell you what you'll do. You go right up to the house and do the churnin'. You just fuss around the house onct and see how you like it. Yes, just march right on up there. The churn's ready, the cream's in it, an' ever'thing. An' see you don't stop till the butter comes, neither.... An' then, Mister Heming, when the churnin's done you can start on them taters, cuttin' 'em up. They're right there on the porch, in the sack. And besides, you can milk the cow this evenin' too, when you git the taters done... Yes, an' ther's suthin' else you kin do. You can git yer own supper this evenin'...ef you expect to git any. Just like to see you gettin' yer own meals onct. So, just go right on. Start to fussin' around in the house, as you call it. The churn's all ready fer you."

Nate stood glaring petulantly at his wife, with a sickly grin playing about the corners of his mouth. At last he turned without saying anything, and started for the house.

And scarcely a half-hour later Sadie Heming went out of the farmlot, following an old gray team and a plow that scudded on the ground before her, raising little puffs of dust about her long swinging skirts.

It was not yet mid-afternoon when Nate burst open the screen door on the back porch and went stumbling and limping in a kind of headlong run across the farmlot toward the little dirt lane that led past a small flaring corn crib and a low hog house to the "tater" field. He could see a gray team moving slowly in the field, and behind the team the tall figure of his wife bending far forward over the handles of the plow. He went straight toward the team, lurching and jerking his body through the plowed soil.

"You get in out a here," he cried, almost in a whine, as he approached the plow. 'I'm goin' to plow my tater field myself. You... you git in out a here."

As the woman looked with some surprise at Nate a broad grin spread slowly about her eyes and mouth. She tossed her head upward and laughed, and the faded blue sunbonnet fell far back on her thick grayish hair.

"Why, I thought you was goin' to do the churnin'," she said, and then laughed again.

"You do yer own churnin'," Nate shouted, "that's what you do, an' leave me alone. I ain't goin' to do yer churnin' fer you. I ain't goin' to do no slavin' fer you, Sadie Heming."

The woman slowly pulled the lines from over her head. "Awright, aww-right," she said almost good humoredly, "just as you say, Mister Heming. Go right ahead and plow it then, since I see you don't like the fussin' around the house so well." Her voice rose, slightly shrill and thin with irony. Then she stepped over onto the plowed ground and stood with one arm akimbo.

The old man's hands shook as he reached for the plow. He was standing in the furrow now, violently jerking and slapping the horses with both lines. As the team moved away he grasped the plow handles fiercely and stumbled on, staring intently at the curling loam beneath him. Once, as he went slowly up the field, he looked backward over his shoulder for an instant, then turned to fix his eyes again on the plow.

When at last he came to the turn of the land much of the anger had left his face. He breathed more freely and easily now. His hands no longer shook so violently. He looked back over the field. The woman was gone—he could see her in the lane, half way to the house already. His eyes fell to the strip of plowed land beside him, and he examined it carefully. Wisps of grass and dried weed stalks showed here and there at the edges of the furrows. "Ughh...look at that. Fine job a plowin' she did... Well, I knowed it. I knowed just what she'd do."

Sadie Heming could hardly see the "eyes" of the potatoes now, in the dusk that was creeping out of the little orchard and gathering slowly around the house. She examined each potato closely before cutting it into sections and dropping them in the pan at her feet. From time to time she looked toward the barn, then gazed uneasily down the lane toward the potato field. Her face was drawn and anxious, but no longer harsh.

At last she poured the potatoes into an empty gunny sack and went out from the porch with a large milk bucket swinging at her side. When she returned, not long afterward, from the direction of the barn, milk froth was spilling over the brim of the bucket onto her dress and her big loose shoes. She stopped for a moment with her hand resting on the little white knob of the screen, and looked again in the direction of the lane before going into the house.

She lit a small oil lamp and set it in its high bracket beside the kitchen window. She set the white oilcloth table with two big blue-rimmed plates, two large glass tumblers, a pitcher of milk, a plate of bread, the pink salt and pepper shakers, the little blue glass full of toothpicks. Then she put the meat and fried potatoes in the "warming oven."

She took her sunbonnet from the back of a chair and suddenly left the kitchen, and the screen door slammed sharply behind her as she walked swiftly toward the little lane leading to the field.

There was still light enough for her to see the horses moving in the field. She walked toward the team, striding heavily through the loose plowed ground, her skirts dragging in the black soil.

"Now, Nate, you better come in out a here," she said as she came up to the plow. "There's no use you stayin' out here all hours like this." The horses suddenly stopped at the sound of her voice, but the driver started to shout at them and to slap their rumps sharply with the lines. The team stood still, however, their heads drooped low over the furrow in front of them.

The woman raised her voice a little higher. "You know you ought to been in out a here an hour ago. Now come on. Onhitch them horses and come on in and git some supper. You ought to be ashamed a this here stubbornness, Nate."—Nate Heming kept staring straight ahead at his team, paying no attention to the woman standing beside the plow. He continued to slap the horses and to shout more and more loudly. His shouting was becoming almost unintelligible, hardly more than a sustained howling and bawling.

At last one of the horses lifted its head and started to move, then the other moved forward also. The jerking and slapping and shouting continued.

Sadie Heming turned to the team and ran up along their side, calling to them to stop. "Whoa...whoa...whoaaa..." She was almost screaming. The horses moved on, very slowly at first, but as the noise behind them increased they went faster, then faster and faster until the plow went forward so rapidly that the driver was forced into a half trot in the furrow behind it. The mingled screaming and shouting followed the team rod after rod up the field.

But at the corner of the land, where the team was swinging at the turn, the woman hurried forward and grasped a bridle rein. One of the horses, then the other came to a full stop, and a few moments afterward they were both drooping their heads over the furrow as before. Gradually the shouting behind the plow lessened, and finally Nate Heming stood, mute with anger, staring at the woman.

"Now you just stop this craziness, Nate Heming," Sadie said when she had got back her breath from the running. "Just you come on in out a here, d'ya understand? Don't be stubborn like this, Nate." Her voice was suddenly not so high or harsh. "You'll make yourself sick, at this kind a work."

The old man still gripped the handles of the plow. He was no longer glaring at the woman. He was looking straight ahead at the horses. He was crying.

The woman moved around to the doubletree and began to unhitch the tugs. Suddenly the old man pulled the lines from around his neck and violently flung them over the plow toward his wife. The buckle struck her cheek, stinging her sharply. Her hand went quickly to her face but she said nothing. She went on with the unhitching.

A few minutes later she was driving the team into the lane that led, now through a deep dusk, toward the house. Once as she went along she thought she could hear Nate's voice, lifted wild and angry behind her. She listened anxiously, but the jangling of the tug chains came clear and sharp in the damp dusk and she could not be sure what he said.

She put the horses in the barn, unharnessed them and fed them. As she came out of the door she saw Nate's figure standing at the corner of the barn. "Ever'thing's done now, Nate. You better come on up to supper." Her voice was quiet and gentle as she spoke. The dark figure at the corner of the barn did not answer.

Halfway to the house she heard a heavy thud behind her, then the jangle of chains. She knew he was rearranging the harness on its wooden pegs. She smiled faintly to herself as she walked on.

In the kitchen she took down the oil lamp from its bracket on the wall and set it on the table, then removed the meat and potatoes from the warming oven. She poured the greasy salt ham onto a white platter and the fried potatoes into a clay colored bowl and set these on the table. Then she stood waiting over beside the window, her face tired and anxious but no longer taut or hard as it had been before.

She had waited for a long time beside the window when the spring on the screen door creaked and someone shuffled across the floor of the back porch. Then Nate appeared in the kitchen door. His face, grimaced against the light, looked very weary and very old. His squinted eyes flickered once or twice as he stared at his wife, and a slight petulant quivering ran along the gray line of his lips. He glanced once at the table, then his eyes lifted again to the woman's face. "Supper's ready, Nate," Sadie Heming said, very quietly, pointing to the table.

"Awright," he said. His lower jaw was shaking violently as he spoke. "You better eat it yourself then. I don't want none a your supper." And he went, swaying, almost headlong through the low door that opened into the unlighted bedroom beyond the kitchen.

Sadie Heming ate very little, some bread and some milk and a few slices of fried potato. Then she cleared the table as noiselessly as possible, but little clinkings and clatterings arose whenever she set a dish away in the cupboard. At every slight noise of the dishes fresh lines would run out from the corner of her mouth, forming tiny pinkish webs under the wisps of grayish hair that had fallen down her cheeks.

When the dishes were done she went out to the porch and returned with a dish pan filled with potatoes which were covered with little white and purplish sprouts. She sat down beside the table and began cutting the potatoes with a small paring knife. Once in a while she would look toward the bedroom. She could see the corner of the great double bed, just visible in the dim light, that fell through the open door from the lamp on the table beside her. She heard sounds from the other room now and again...the quiet slap of a suspender falling against a trouser leg, the hard clap of a shoe upon the floor, the crackle of soil-caked overalls flung over a chair...then the creak of a bed slat. The cutting of the potatoes went on again, steadily, and there was no sound now except the lisp of the knife cutting through the soft flesh of the potatoes.

A loud heavy breathing came from the bedroom. It grew very loud and very slow, the labored breathing of a tired, exhausted body. The woman stopped the cutting, with half of a large potato held before her in her hand. She cut it in two pieces, then dropped these in the pan. She put the knife on the table beside her and let her hands fall in the hollow of her lap, then sat for a long while listening to the heavy breathing in the other room. At last she rose suddenly and impulsively from her chair and went quickly over to the door where she stood gazing into the darkened room. Her head was dropped slightly forward and she seemed to be looking down at the bed dimly showing in the light that fell over her stooping shoulder from the high lamp on the kitchen wall behind her. Once or twice her shoulders and her head shook convulsively but slightly, as though she were crying. After some time she turned slowly from the door and came back to her chair, where she sat down and with fumbling fingers took off her heavy shoes. She went very quietly back to the door again, but stopped there as before. For a long while she stood gazing into the half-dark of the farther room. Her shoulders no longer trembled. She seemed very quiet now. Finally her hand began playing idly with the fastening of her dress, and she moved as if to go through the door. Then she turned abruptly and came back toward the lamp in its high bracket against the kitchen wall. As she reached up for the lamp her broad, rough face showed wet and shiny against the light, and the line of her tight narrow lips was broken and softened in a faint smile. She blew the light out, and went through the sudden darkness of the kitchen toward the heavy breathing in the other room.

12.

BLACK-PURPLE IN THE CORN

There was a darker shade of green in the corn this morning. Yesterday it was just like it had been the day before, and the day before. But this morning the fields were a darker color, as Sel Ganer looked out over the prairie from where he stood, one hand holding to an iron brace, leaning against the windmill.

Out of the prairie distances it came to him, this new mood, this subtly new color of the fields—a hint of black-purple in the corn. A new richness, a maturity, a fullness of growth in the broad oil-green blades. The wonderful plethoric languor of it all drifted into the man's spirit as he looked out at the fields through the lashes of his half-closed eyes. Vaguely he felt a sense of merited leisure, a deep, quiet realization of labors finished. For now the cornplowing was done for the season—those interminable weeks of plowing and plowing up and down the fields.

At last Sel Ganer remembered the white jug beside him. What he had come to the windmill for was to get a morning's supply of water before he should go out to the hayfield. He was going onto the mower this morning, for the hay was just ready to be cut. The haying would not be monotonous, endless, like the cornplowing had been. He did not mind the haying much.

He picked up the white jug by the old hame strap that was

fastened to its looped handle. He had filled it a good quarter of an hour ago, before he had started to look at the cornfields—and had forgotten it since.... Then he moved off toward the barn to get his team for the mowing.

"You got everythin' now?" asked Sel's father, who came through the farmyard gate with two buckets of milk as Sel started to open the door of the barn.

"Yeah, everythin'."

"How's the sickle?"

"Sickle's all right, I guess. Sharpened it the other day, and hain't mowed nothin' much with it since."

Sel reached over the barn door and unhooked the latch. The elder Ganer, a little old man with soft, quiet eyes, and a heedless stumbling way of walking, hurried off to where the mower stood in a corner of the barnyard.

"Guess it'll do," he said, coming back from the mower as Sel was leading his second horse out of the barn. "Could be a little sharper, but guess it'll do. Hain't got much time for sharpenin' it, anyways. We got to get into that hay pretty quick, the way it looks. Gettin' pretty ripe in places."

"Yeah, wouldn't wonder." Sel led his horses over to the other corner of the barn where the watering tank stood; a few minutes later he was hitching his team to the mower. Then he went out of the gate with the white jug hanging from the hames of one of the horses.

As Sel Ganer rode along the back pasture lane the corn came up to the fence beside him. Once or twice his horses tried to reach their heads over the fence as they walked along, hungry for a bite of the dark green blades. He was vaguely pleased by the heavy odor of the corn and by the dark green walls that crowded up to the fence on both sides of him. He could see down the rows as he passed, and underneath, the dry gray soil was dark with almost uniform shadow cast by the big green blades above.

Once he stopped the team, raised himself on the mower seat, and looked out over the corn. He could hear the horses tearing the blades from the stalks near the fence, but he let them go on eating, while he kept gazing over the dark green field flashing in the sun everywhere about him. At last he sat down on his mower, backed the team away from the wire fence, slapped the lines carelessly on their glistening ramps and moved idly on toward the meadow.

13.

THE RAIN

He kept staring through the window against which the rain was beating. Between the little streams rushing and mingling downward over the glass, he watched the apple tree in the yard. Its thin top branches bent and swayed under the wind and the rain, as great sheets of water swooped and bellied slantingly out of a sky he could nowhere see, flinging themselves headlong over the trees and the barn and the blurred grayness of the land beyond.

Something seemed suddenly to twist and tighten all the lines of his face, and the rough, hard cheeks were lifted until little wrinkles pushed themselves up against the sockets of his eyes.

Here it was the first, of May, and nary a furrow ploughed in the fields... He ought to been in the fields two weeks ago...

His gaze fixed itself upon the upper branches of the apple tree, and a little while later it went out straining through the swinging rain that hid, then revealed the gray-black fields behind the barn.

Suddenly the paint brush in his lifted hand shifted and fell slightly backwards. He felt it pressing heavily against the butt of his thumb. He looked down at the sticky greenish thing drooping from his fingers.

The painting began again, with intermittent swishing and slapping sounds. Ligg Morrisy was stooping beneath the window, beside the baseboard that ran along the edge of blue and yellow linoleum. As he went on painting he lifted his left hand automatically and rested it on the window sill.

After some time the swishing and slapping stopped, and the man rose to look intently out the window again. Two or three green finger prints showed on the dull yellow of the window sill at his knees.

The twisted lines still pressed up against his eyes, which, between their narrowed lids, were as dull and gray as the tree and the barn and the land beyond.

He heard a faint rustling behind him. The rustling came close to him, and yet it seemed far behind him still, separate and distant, and far away from him, and far away from the rushing of the wind outside and the hollow rattle of rain against the window. There was a pressure at his arm. He stepped slightly aside.

The face of his wife, pink and flushed against the grayness, looked up at him around the smooth curve of his shoulder.

"Ligg, what are you doing?" The voice was suddenly sharp and close in his ear. "Just look at them marks on that sill... Ligg... Oh, why don't you look at what you're doing?"

Before he could answer she had rustled away and was back with an oily rag, rubbing the paint marks from the sill. He saw her dark head nodding and shaking over the sill. She was gone again. He gazed out as before at the silver blur of rain and land. The silver had grown darker. It seemed very bluish and very cold.

Vaguely he heard the clacking and clattering behind him...then the deadened bang of an oil stove lid...a hard metallic scraping and tapping... The noises became vaguer still, very remote and very far behind him. Then he heard only the rain sweeping past the window.

He remembered the oats sowing. He had got it in in good shape this spring. Dark green in spots, even two weeks ago. His eyes widened and brightened momentarily, then became dull and narrow as before as he again began peering intently through the cold, blue window.

Suddenly the rain came in streaming, beating torrents, completely hiding the barn and the land...

He thought of the corn, and his mind was instantly sharp and clear...not a furrow ploughed anywhere in the fields. His face was again a mask, in which the wrinkles crawled and twisted and then settled, very hard and deep, under his eyes.

After a while—it seemed a very long while—he heard the woman talking to him from the kitchen. She was saying something about getting done before supper. He felt the paint sticky and clammy between his fingers. He lifted his head stiffly and peered more intently through the rain, but he was thinking about the voice out in the kitchen... Just what she wanted, fussing around inside the house...him in out of the fields, painting and cleaning. She didn't seem to care about things... She never thought about the corn... He heard the rain still pouring against the window...

He went out to the kitchen and silently put the paint bucket under a table, then picked up a crumpled hat and a coat from behind the stove. It was dry and stiff. As he put on the coat he mumbled something about doing the chores. A sharp hard rattle of the doorknob, and the man went quickly out into the storm.

As he crossed to the barn the rain beat at him, pressing the clothes against his body. But it came in unsteady sweeps now, not so heavily as he had seen it falling all afternoon. As he stood reaching for the latch inside the feedway door the wind seemed to cease suddenly. For a moment there was a hush in the air about him. He heard the hollow pecking of raindrops on the crown of his hat. Then the wind came again in a quick violent gust, blowing the rain against the side of his face as he stepped into the barn.

He heard the startled whimpering and neighing of horses as he stumbled through the hay in the feedway. The corn felt firm and hard and strangely dry in his hands, when he dropped it into the feedboxes. He heard the horses munching and fumbling the ears in the boxes.

When he came to the feedway door again the rain was blowing, thin and fine, between the barn and the house. It was hardly more than a heavy mist now, shifting and tossing wildly on the wind. And the wind itself was not so fierce or steady. Between gusts, it seemed to stop and gasp at the corners of the barn. As he stood for a minute or two in the door, his wet face shiny in the dusk, he knew the storm was broken.

Then far past the apple tree and the low roof of the house he saw a finger of red light pushing itself along the wet bluish fields. It was a cold, limpid red, like flame seen a through ice. Slowly it spread and widened, livid at its center and green and purple and gold along the shifting edges of the clouds. Then his gaze came back to the little house. Its roof was wet and shiny in the reflected light. The apple tree had become a great round patch of crimson lace with darker ribs of trunk and upper limbs.

As he walked slowly toward the house the rent of dead flame moved upward in zig-zag slashes, and the clouds above it shifted and pulled gradually apart. Before he had got to the house little patches of deep blue, fringed with pink, had appeared in the upper sky. He stood for a while with a hand resting on the knob, his face reflecting the dull red glow, before turning indifferently and pushing the door inward with his shoulder.

As he stepped into the kitchen his eye fell upon the two shiny red handles of the warming ovens. Even the fat black curve of the pipe above the stove glowed dully in the light that poured through the uncurtained window and filled the little room.

His wife was bending over the oil-cloth table near the window, pouring fried potatoes from a skillet into a small white bowl. Loose strands of her hair had been turned to fine gold by the fight from the window.

"Through?" she asked, without turning.

"Yeah, all through," Ligg said, dropping a wet coat and hat behind the stove. The woman began scraping some scorched potatoes from the bottom of the skillet. He went on into the dining room, to the window. The apple tree and the barn were now in a dead, even light. Farther away the greening oat fields had been changed into a thin frail gold... Maybe he could get to plowing in a few days, by end of the week anyway... If he could get somebody...like Tob Jennings... Put a gang and a sulky into it, wouldn't take so long... Yeah, ought to get Tob or somebody...

He heard the rustling of a dress behind him, then the sound of a dish pushed across the cloth on the table.

"Here, come on now, supper's ready... Ligg." His wife's voice was light and careless, the way it always was when she was busy. Usually he didn't like to hear her talk that way, but now he didn't seem to mind it.

Once, when he was reaching for the potatoes his eyes noticed green rawish paint around his finger nails, but he only stared absently at it for a moment. The woman talked almost constantly through the meal..."blue...think light blue would be better for the kitchen...papering...seen some awful nice pink and green designs in at Norton's the other Saturday...bedroom needs it pretty bad too..." He heard her voice running on carelessly, without ever seeming to stop.

If he could get Tob. Tob could do the harrowin' too. Wouldn't want to put Tob on the planter... Want to make sure of a good check in corn... He took another piece of salt ham.

He could hear the woman's voice...still something about papering...but the voice seemed to stay on the other side of the table, where the woman was...at times he did not hear it at all. Once in a while, when she bent over her plate, he noticed how white and thin and straight was the part that ran back in the middle of her dark hair...

He pushed away from the table, moving the chair alternately on its two hind legs, then tilted himself back against the wall. Absently he watched and heard the woman clearing the table, while he pulled a pipe from his pocket with an awkward swaying and hunching of shoulders. The smoke came regularly in whitish, faintly bluish clouds, and he watched each of these intently until it disappeared.

He was thinking that he had better go over and see Tob the first thing in the morning... Yeah, sulky and gang together...that was what he'd better do.

14.

WHERE DADDY WAS LOOKING

I remember our other house so well. It was very small and low, and there wasn't any floor. Only just the ground. It seemed so hot inside, and my eyes hurt when it got hot that way, especially after supper. But outside it was always cold over at our other house. There were big trees everywhere, without any leaves on them. The trees always seemed so still. Some of the trees were almost black, and some were silver and shiny and everywhere under the trees there was always snow.

But I remember the day the snow was all gone, and I heard the birds in the stillness outside. Only, the trees were all dark and silver yet. Then I remember how Daddy came home with the horses and the big wagon. He brought the horses and wagon right up to the house. When he came in he told Mother he guessed we could go, and he was laughing all the time he was talking. Then Daddy started taking everything outside and putting it in the big wagon, even the table and stove and the big bed and everything. But I couldn't understand because Mother wasn't laughing at all. Mother didn't say hardly anything, even when' she was helping Daddy put little things like her kettle and pans in the wagon.

When we went away in the big wagon I was between Daddy and Mother on the table that Daddy had put way up in front of the wagon. The sack of straw that Daddy had put on the table for me and

Mother wasn't big enough, so Daddy only sat on the table. But after a while the straw seemed awful hard, and it made me wriggle sometimes. But Mother didn't seem to move at all. She just watched the road, and she held me very tight when the wagon jumped and the big wheels made loud, hard noises right down under us.

But Daddy was laughing and shouting at the horses. He kept laughing almost all the time, and he shouted awful loud sometimes, like the horses couldn't hear. But I knew that they could hear. Horses can hear even better than Daddy, or me, or anybody.

Sometimes Daddy looked down at me, and brought his big red face right down to mine and laughed and told me not to be afraid and asked me if I didn't like to ride on the big wagon. After that he would sit away up above me and take the long whip and crack it loud and quick away out over the horses' backs. He never hit the horses hard with the whip, but just cracked it. I liked Daddy because he wouldn't hit the horses. Sometimes I laughed when Daddy cracked the whip awful hard. Daddy would look down at me and laugh too. And then he would go on cracking the whip just to make me laugh. But other times Daddy just hummed to himself, and then he seemed to forget about the whip and the horses, and even me and Mother. He just looked away up the road that kept going on through the still gray trees that came so close up to us everywhere.

After a long time we came out of the big trees. It was like all at once. And there was the river. Everywhere out before us was the shiny water. I could feel Mother sitting very stiff then and she was holding me so tight it almost hurt. When I looked up at her, her face was awful white, and she was looking out at the river very hard. But Daddy only looked down and he was laughing at me and Mother.

Then Daddy was standing up very tall in the wagon, and he was speaking to the horses. Only very low, not loud like before. And he didn't crack the whip over them at all. I could see the lines going down from Daddy's hands to the horses. The lines were very tight and straight. And then Daddy was bracing himself. I felt his knee pressing very hard on my leg. All at once the horses were stepping into the water. There were big splashes down under the horses' bellies. When I saw the wheels going down into the water I was so afraid I thought I couldn't breathe. All the time Mother was holding me tighter and tighter. And now I could see the dark green water going faster and faster under the horses right through the big wheels down under us.

We kept going down into the water deeper and deeper. Then all at once I heard Daddy talking to the horses. He was talking louder and louder. He was almost shouting. The wagon seemed bending and twisting and I could hear it cracking all the time. The water kept going faster and faster. It was green and shiny everywhere around us. Down underneath I heard it making loud sucking sounds all the time.

Then I heard Daddy shouting. He was shouting even louder than before. We were going up out of the water. The wagon went in jumps right after the horses. I remember how the horses' backs dropped real low just before every jump, and how their legs looked with the big muscles standing away out and running up and down and all their skin so wet and dark. Only, in under the harness there were little white places too.

But all at once there were shiny little rocks and pebbles, everywhere under the horses' legs and the wagon. I looked up at Daddy and we were stopped, and he was looking down at me and Mother. Then Daddy started to laugh. He stooped away down and patted Mother's head on her black fascinator. I thought Mother was crying at first. But when I looked up at Mother's face I could tell she was only trembling and laughing and smiling up at Daddy. Then Daddy and Mother both looked down at me together, and I laughed too and after that I saw them looking at each other. Only Mother wasn't laughing like Daddy. She was just laughing a little, and very low.

Daddy was looking back at the river then, away up over the wagon. I wanted to look back at the river too. But the big stove was right behind me and I couldn't see at all except through a little hole. When I looked hard I could see the river, but it didn't look dark and green like when we were going through the water. It looked very bright and silver. I thought it seemed like Daddy's eyes when he bent down so close. But Mother didn't look back at the river at all. She only said we'd better go on for it was a long way yet.

Daddy started the wagon then. We went on over the bright sand and the shiny pebbles. We went up very steep, past bushes and big rocks. And there were more trees that kept coming right up to the road like before. I could hear the horses breathing awful hard sometimes. They smelled too. But I didn't care. I knew the horses were very tired.

Then Daddy was shouting "Whoa" very loud, and all at once the trees were gone. Daddy was standing away up in the wagon now. I saw he was looking far away over the horses' heads, and he wasn't talking or laughing at all. I looked away where he was looking. I had never looked so far before, all at once. There weren't any trees anywhere. Just tiny little trees and houses very far off. They seemed away way off, and they were all by themselves.

When I looked up at Daddy's face again he laughed very quick and then reached down and picked me up and put me, on his shoulder. I could feel his big hands holding my legs very hard. I looked out where Daddy was looking for a long time. I had never seen anything so big and good like this. I told Daddy that, leaning down. Daddy laughed very quick and danced me on his shoulder. After that he put me down beside Mother again.

When I looked up at Mother I saw her looking far away too. I knew Mother was very tired, the way her eyes looked in behind the black fascinator. But her face kept smiling all the time and she was looking out where Daddy was.

Then Daddy reached down and took his big whip and cracked it up near the horses' heads. The wagon started so quick I almost fell back against the stove, but Mother caught me and held me tight like she did before. After awhile Daddy sat down beside me and Mother again. Then he let the big whip hang down behind the horses. Daddy didn't laugh or talk to the horses now or crack his whip or anything. I could see he wasn't sad though, the way his mouth looked in between the whiskers on his face, and the way his eyes looked too, not bright and sparkly any more like the water back in the river, but just quiet and glad. After a while I wondered why Daddy stayed so quiet that way.

Sometimes we passed big houses, only one was a yellow house and it was even bigger than the white houses. Behind the yellow house there was a big yellow barn and behind the other houses there were red barns. But one of the barns was old and black looking, and it had a kind of caved-in back. There were big trees around some of the houses and barns.

I remember once we met some men in a wagon. You could only see their heads and shoulders because the wagon was very high, and the men wore big gray caps, but not like Daddy's. Daddy was wearing my old gray cap, with the hole in the top where the tassle used to be. The men drove their big wagon away out to the side of the road to let us pass. Then they waved at Daddy and Daddy waved back and shouted at the men. After that Daddy was very glad. He kept cracking his whip very loud all the time.

The road went very straight, and I could see it away out very far in front of the horses. We passed other houses, only they weren't so big like before. I kept looking away off in front mostly. I wanted to see where Daddy was looking. My eyes got very tired trying to see where Daddy could.

Then after a long time I knew it was beginning to get dark. Kind of all at once, I knew it. It seemed like the darkness was mostly closer to us. Away off it was all brightness yet, like a great fire. And there were little trees and a house standing in the fire. Only they weren't burning at all. It was like they were very blue and dark, and the brightness was everywhere behind them.

I could tell Daddy was looking out at the great fire all the time. And when I twisted back, I could see Mother was looking at the fire too. I tried to keep looking very hard where Daddy and Mother were. Only, my eyes were getting so tired now. I could barely see the little blue trees and the house standing in the fire. They seemed to get very dark after a while. Then the fire wasn't so big either, like before. The darkness seemed to be coming everywhere, very slow. It was coming right up to us all the time. My eyes were awful tired now. After that it seemed like I couldn't see anything but the horses. I heard their funny clumping noises away down the road. They seemed to be going into more and more darkness all the time.

When I woke up it was dark all around me. I was so afraid I didn't move. I didn't even breathe. But all at once I knew I was in Daddy's and Mother's big bed, and I thought I was in our old house. Only it was so dark and funny. Then I saw a door down below the big bed, and the door was all bright, and I could see into another room and that was all bright too. I could see Mother's lamp sitting on a table out in the other room. I heard Daddy and Mother talking then. Sometimes Daddy laughed real low. But mostly they just kept on talking. I tried to listen, but I couldn't hear what Daddy and Mother were saying at all. After a while they seemed to be talking farther away. And then Daddy was laughing. Just like he did back at the river, and cracking his big whip, and I was laughing too. We were up on the big straight road all at once. We were looking into the brightness. And now Daddy was laughing all the time...away off...in the brightness...

15.

RUST IN THE WHEAT

After pulling the four tired horses around the narrow, pointed corner, Mart Conway stopped the binder, turned in the high iron seat and shouted to a pair of shockers far behind him. "Might as well go on in, boys. No need a-waitin' for me. I'll just go on cuttin' till it's all down."

The two men finished the shock they were working at and moved slowly across the stubble in the direction of a lane that led from the field.

The man on the binder turned his team into the wheat again. Only about an acre of grain remained standing, a small island in the middle of the big field. As he went up the side of the little land he kept tripping the bundle carrier at regular intervals with his foot, dropping the sheaves in even windrows along the field. His eyes caught the reflection of red light on the toe of his shoe each time his foot lifted at the lever, and he could see it shining along the two thin reins that sloped away from his hand toward the horses.

Once in a while he looked away over the field. The shocks in the distance were getting darker now, indistinct except where the sun glowed red on the tops of them. Mart could see that they were not thick—"nuthin' like other years," he said to himself. He reached forward, touched the tired off horse with the long whip, then put it back in its socket beside him, while the lash went bobbing jerkily along in the glowing air above his head.

He felt it getting cooler as he rode along; and he was glad, for it would make it easier on the team. A heavy dampness was settling over the field. The hum of the binder grew loud and hollow in the still evening. The grain was becoming tough, for the sickle pounded and clattered with a dull sound that penetrated the constant moan of driving gears and chains and canvases. The tired horses went more slowly, rounding the sharp corners in wide, lagging sweeps. Sometimes Mart talked almost gently to his team. "Jim…Nance…in there now…just a little more, 'nother round or two…come on, boys, in there now." Two or three times at the corners he lifted the long whip and touched a rump lightly with the lash.

He wished he could get the rest of it cut in a hurry. The horses were very tired. He could see their heads drooping lower as they nodded slowly onward. He noticed their broad shiny backs, swinging under the harness, their breeching shifting with their stride, and the smears of greasy lather on their wet legs where the tugs touched. He felt the weariness of his horses in his own body, the ache and strain of their terrific pulling.

Once as he was moving down the side of the small land, the binder choked in the wet grain. Mart got down from his high iron seat and worked with the lower elevator canvas, jerking angrily at the matted straw. When he climbed back upon the binder, the dark, wet lines around his armpits were darker still with the powdered rust from the grain.

The corners were so pointed now that the horses had to make wide, sweeping reverse turns, stumbling over each other's hoofs as they dragged the binder back into the grain. Only two or three full swaths were left, and the cutting would be done. When at last these were down, a long whisp of grain still remained standing. Mart turned his four horses at the corner and the binder, running almost empty, moaned loudly as it went up the field, neatly clipping the thin strip of wheat.

After wrapping the lines around one of the high levers, Mart Conway stepped awkwardly over the twine box on the ground. He looked thoughtfully at the binder for a while, his face already relaxed from the long strain of the cutting. "Wish I could truck her up tonight," he said. Then a slight, grim pucker came into his lips, and he shook his head a little. "Can't do it by myself, though."

He walked slowly around the binder toward the team and began to throw the tugs over their wet backs. And a little while later he went off across the field through the dusk that was swiftly falling. He picked his way deviously among the shocks, driving one team, leading the other horses behind him, with the two jockey sticks under his arm. As he walked along, he heard the switching of the horses' hoofs through the clipped stubble. His sweaty shirt grew cold and clammy on his shoulders, and he felt the air come damp against his brow. But whenever his eyes wandered from the horses, he noticed a slight pinkish glow now touching only the cap-sheaves of the shocks.

As he drove out of the field into the lane that ran up past the cornfield and the alfalfa meadow toward the house, he stopped and went back to close the heavy gate. Then he stood for a while with one hand resting on the top plank, gazing back over the field.

"Won't make much," he said quietly to himself. "Fifteen or twenty, I reckon. Never seen rust so bad... Well, glad I got it all down, anyway."

The last pale hint of the sunset had left the field, and now the most distant shocks were only splotches of darker shadow against the dusk of the stubble. Far away beyond the low hedge on the Biggs place the west was still red, but its color seemed removed from the world, no longer touching even the farthest edges of the prairie. Motionless and stark, the binder off in the field lifted its black, humped form into the cold glow of the sky.

For a minute or two Mart Conway stood looking into the west. Then he turned slowly, picked up the reins and the jockey sticks, and went homeward through the shadows that crept out of the cornfield into the narrow lane.

16.

BICYCLE BUILT FOR TWO

Eliakim Brown had learned one thing well. He had spent fifty-seven years making sure that nothing ever changes for the better. Other facts just didn't seem to matter to him. He didn't seem interested, for instance, even in the fact that everybody around Plovers Run had been smiling at him for years, and especially on band concert nights when he came into town driving his fat gray mare, always with the widow Dodge beside him in the buggy. Eliakim knew what he knew and seemed satisfied; if nobody else ever learned it, that was none of his worry. He was sure of this one truth, that things never change for the better.

This explained Eliakim Brown's clothes, his diet, his talk, his way of farming, everything. Above all, it explained the widow Dodge and the place she took in his life. Every Wednesday night, through the whole summer, and this for the past twelve of fifteen years, he had stopped at her place with his horse and buggy, and taken her, dressed in a full blue dress and a faded green hat, to the band concert up at Plovers Run. Everybody had watched the weekly spectacle impatiently. Even the widow, who was once plump and talkative, had grown thinner from puzzlement and doubt, and more and more silent from a long habit of keeping both ears cocked on soft Wednesday evenings for the question that never passed Eliakim's lips.

Of course Mickey Collins had explained it all to everybody in Plovers Run, but nobody believed him any more. Mickey had lived between Eliakim and the widow on the old south County Road. For years he had insisted on helping both Eliakim and the widow with their farming—exchanging help, he had ambiguously called it. He had played the double part of matrimonial agent and reporter to the community at large. He was always telling the widow how miserably alone and helpless was Eliakim; he explained the lonely life of the widow to Eliakim while they were haying or butchering or picking corn together. The widow listened with softened eyes; Eliakim only went on working as if he had hardly heard; it was the difference between innocence and philosophy. But Mickey, being on the side of love, was ingenious; he was constantly announcing the marriage to everybody except Eliakim and the widow. "Sure they're goin' to get married. Pretty soon. The widow as good as admitted it the other day. Eliakim won't deny it neither." Mickey was always positive, absolute. Only after years did the community become thoroughly skeptical. Mickey Collins was a liar in the interests of love and its essential madness. Plovers Run knew this now, and forgave him, even continued listening to him, wishing it could still believe.

Others, too, had done all they could for the widow. There was Sam Lewellyn. Sam was the Ford agent in Plovers Run, and he was the leader of the band. Nobody could play the cornet like Sam, nor sell half so many cars. Sam had taken over the Ford agency when he gave up the livery barn ten years ago. Back in the days of the livery 'barn Eliakim and Sam had been very good friends of a sort. Eliakim had bought his fat gray driving mare from Sam. In those days Eliakim used frequently to stop in the barn for a chat, on rainy days, on Saturday afternoons, in the fall, or Sundays. Since Sam had turned the livery barn into a garage, however, Eliakim had never been there. Eliakim Brown stood staunchly on that. He would have nothing to do with automobiles. Everybody might buy cars that wanted to, and Sam Lewellyn had indeed sold a Ford to practically every farmer in the community. Eliakim kept his fat driving mare. She was his strong link with the truth. She preserved the one great certitude. When things changed, it was always for the worse. Folks would learn, maybe, Eliakim said. But most likely they'd learn too late, by breaking their necks. Spending their last cent just to ride around in one of those fancy gigs Sam Lewellyn was selling.

But of course Sam had tried. He had repeatedly asked Eliakim if he wasn't in the market for a Ford, being always careful to put the proposition jokingly, in the old indifferent manner of a horse-trader. He had stopped Eliakim on the street on rainy afternoons; had mentioned the matter to him, very gaily, during the intermissions on band concert evenings; had even gone out to Eliakim's place once. Only a born salesman like Sam would have had the nerve to go on trying, after seeing Eliakim's hard eyes and hearing him say, time and again, that he'd as leave think of breaking his neck outright as getting one of those fancy gigs to do it for him. It wasn't even a decent, honest way for a man to go about killing himself.

Sam and Mickey Collins had of course talked it over many times. They even made a kind of game out of it, or a partnership in which Mickey was to get half the commission when the Ford was sold. Sam remained strictly the business man, repeating his proposition whenever he saw Eliakim. Mickey simply let his feelings guide him, and they told him to use the widow. During haying time he would casually mention to Eliakim the fact that the widow Dodge had never once ridden in an automobile. He would even say that she had remarked this to him when he had last seen her, the day he was over there helping her hired man to ring the pigs. And then he would say something about women being foolish about such things. They were always wanting new and fancy things, though of course it was not so unreasonable in the widow Dodge. She didn't have the chances of some women. She lived a lonely life, a very lonely life. But to all this Eliakim Brown was silent. A few times, when Mickey had talked this way during the haying, Eliakim had stuck his fork in the ground and looked strangely off at the sky. But he never once said anything. And the following Wednesday night Eliakim would, as usual, take Lena Dodge to the band concert with the fat gray mare and the buggy. He would find her the same as always before. She would be beaming at him when he arrived at the wicket gate. Her bright gentle face, broadening till it suggested the plumpness that was gone, her stiff gay laugh that answered his invariable invitation to the band concert, and even, when she had climbed into the buggy beside him, the slightest hint of perfume on her ample bosom—these were complete reassurance. Eliakim Brown coughed awkwardly and drove away and knew that the widow had not changed for the worse.

It was in late June that the dreadful discovery was made. The alfalfa haying was finished, and the corn would soon be laid by for the summer. The widow was riding to the concert this evening, as usual. She sensed that something was wrong. She saw it out of the corner of an eye, in the stiff face of Eliakim Brown beside her. It seemed like a fixed hardness in his lips, a glassy stare in his eyes, an indefinable, straining prominence in his brow. Lena knew that Eliakim had changed, and it was terrible. She was sure that Eliakim's heart had hardened, that he loved her no more, or if at all, with a less ardent love.

Even Mickey Collins saw the same thing the next morning, when he went over to Eliakim's place. There was a painful sternness upon Eliakim's brow, a change in his face that was undeniable. Mickey did not want to believe what was suddenly all too plain. He did not want to think of Eliakim's brow as a casket enclosing a dead love. It was too strange, so strange that it actually left Mickey awed and silent at first. He said nothing to anybody about it. With a sinking heart he went on telling stories to neighbors about Eliakim's growing devotion to the widow. It was the first time in years that he had served the widow ignobly.

But two days later his tongue was suddenly loosed. His heart was full with joy. His lips actually opened into rapturous song. For he was hurrying across the fields, just at dusk, with what was to be both the sweetest and the saddest news that the widow Dodge had heard in years. He had just left Eliakim's place. Eliakim Brown was in bed with a raging fever, and he had asked Mickey Collins to bring the widow Dodge at once.

Darkness was gathering as Mickey led the happy, weeping woman through the fields. Above her panting sobs as she ran, Mickey's voice rose insistently. He was telling her to be brave, to be worthy of the great, yearning heart of Eliakim Brown. At last they stood just outside Eliakim's door. The widow waited, desperately trying to control her sobbing breath. After a few moments she felt of her hair, instinctively. She was slowly shocked into realizing that she had forgotten her green hat. She remembered that Eliakim had never seen her without it. And then she knew that her hair had fallen wildly about her head, that her dress hung limp and wet upon her sweating shoulders and bosom. For a moment her face lengthened in despair. Then her eyes flashed fearlessly and passionately before her. She leaped forward, running, her arms stretched out before her. With an anguished wail she burst through the screen door. Her weeping voice went echoing through all the rooms of the house. Mickey Collins followed her now, creeping through the door. He went stealthily toward the sound of the widow's sobbing and wailing that was now coming out from the side bedroom. He peered cautiously into the room. It was dimly lighted by a kerosene lamp on a low dresser. The widow Dodge was on her knees beside the bed. Her hot wet arm was thrown across Elikiam's breast, just above the dark line of the bed clothes. Eliakim's breast and shoulders were covered by a blue work shirt. The widow's tangled hair lay upon the grayish white of the pillow, beside Eliakim's long fixed face. Her spluttering sobs were now shaking the whole bed until the galluses of Eliakim's trousers were tapping lightly against the dark wooden bedhead where they hung.

Eliakim Brown's eyes were burning up toward the low ceiling of the room. His long red face, beside the widow's tangled hair, was that of a man rapt out of himself. He was beginning to speak now, trying to keep a nervous tremble out of his voice. He was telling Lena Dodge that she was to have everything. He had made the will years ago, and she was to get all—the farm, the house, the furniture, his personal effects, even his gold watch. And she was to have the gray mare. Eliakim's voice became almost soft and reverent as he mentioned the mare. And how he was silent, his eyes burning fiercely and rapturously at the ceiling as before. Lena's only answer was another fit of sobbing that shook the bed more violently than before. Slowly one of Eliakim's hands reached out from the bed clothes until it rested upon the widow's dark head. At last the sobbing and shaking of the bed began to subside. Then Mickey Collins crept quickly out of the house. A madness seemed to possess him as he ran singing and shouting homeward across the fields.

In the slow weeks that followed Plovers Run held its breath, listening to Mickey Collins as he talked on and on. The widow Dodge was nursing Eliakim Brown back to life, virtually pulling him back from the edge of the grave. Though greatly pleased. Plovers Run was not much surprised by this. It had faith in the primitive, healing force of the widow's passion. It only wondered, slightly, that Mickey Collins could thus be proved, at last, such a prophet even in his own township.

By the end of July Eliakim Brown was up and around the farm. For the past week now, the widow had been returning home of nights, usually escorted by Mickey Collins. She only came over during the day to see that Eliakim's meals were properly prepared. And by the end of the first week in August it was confidently announced by Mickey Collins that Eliakim and the widow would be present at the band concert on the following Wednesday evening. But even Mickey did not know the full meaning of his announcement. He was to learn that love is, after all, many mysterious things, and that, even he was really only a man of little faith.

It was just before dawn on the following Monday that Eliakim stopped at Lena's gate with the buggy and gray mare and then started with the widow for the county seat. They were married there, at high noon. It all happened so quietly that no one, not Mickey Collins himself, was aware of anything unusual.

That night Mr. and Mrs. Eliakim Brown returned by way of the old dirt road on the eastern hills, stopping at Plovers Run on their way home. Eliakim had a brief mysterious conversation with Sam Lewellyn, the most friendly talk that he and Sam had had since the days of the livery barn. It was long after dark, but with the moon shining full upon them, that Eliakim and Lena passed Mickey Collins's place. Mickey heard them and was wonderstruck. In the strong moonlight he could see their faces as they drove past on the road, for the buggy top, for the first time in Mickey's memory, was dropped back. He could see the unearthly whiteness of their two faces in the blue-green light. Mickey actually rubbed both his eyes, then looked again. But there were the two faces, moving as in a dream. Mickey Collins suddenly felt ashamed of himself, and somehow disappointed and very unimportant.

It was not until the evening of the next day—Tuesday—that Mickey and Plovers Run knew the whole truth. At two o'clock in the afternoon Sam Lewellyn drove out of Plovers Run in a new Ford coupe, after leaving instructions to one of his garage hands to follow him an hour later in one of the "demonstrators." Sam drove straight out the South County Road toward Eliakim Brown's place. Half an hour later Eliakim was beginning his first lesson in driving an automobile. He was driving the new Ford away from his front gate, with Sam Lewellyn beside him, while Lena was waving him luck from the steps of the front porch.

The Ford coupe came to a jerking stop in front of Eliakim's house about two hours later. Eliakim stepped awkwardly out from under the wheel, and now he was shaking hands with Sam, nervously but heartily. They stood talking and grinning at each other for a little while. Just as Sam finally turned to get into the other car that the mechanic had brought out, Eliakim pulled a cigar from an inner pocket and offered it to him with a stiff flourish. He backed away toward the yard gate, grinning broadly as Sam drove off. Sam waved and shouted backward out of a cloud of dust. As Eliakim walked slowly over the lawn toward the house, Lena was waiting for him on the porch steps, her hands pressed together on her bosom. She was leaning far out from the porch, like one ready to fall forward in a swoon.

By this time Mickey Collins had come down from his windmill, which he had been using as an observation tower, and was out in the road desperately waving Sam Lewellyn to a stop. Sam told the whole truth, calling fluent curses upon himself if it weren't the truth. After Sam had driven away, Mickey stood in the dusty road for a long time, bareheaded and silent, growing more and more reverent before the mysterious facts of life. He was wearing for once, the badge of absolute sincerity. He was grinning, in a very foolish, chastened way, down at his toes.

Everywhere in Plovers Run, Sam's news brought the same foolish grin. It was not till the next day—Wednesday—that the town recovered from its surprise. By noon it was able to begin thinking of immediate, practical things. There would be a band concert that evening, and as Sam was telling everybody, Mr. and Mrs. Eliakim Brown would be there in their new Ford. By early afternoon Sam had recruited helpers, and was decorating the band stand that stood in the middle of Main Street. All the flags and bunting that had been used on the Fourth of July were got out again. By evening the wooden stand was striped in red and white and blue and spangled with great stars. The cars were beginning to come in. Ben Parker, with his marshal's badge pinned to one of his blue suspenders, was showing people where to park the cars along the street. Plovers Run was ready for the band concert, and ready for Eliakim and Lena Brown when they would arrive in the flashing new coupe. According to instructions from Sam Lewellyn and several of the business men, Ben Parker was reserving a place for Eliakim Brown's Ford in the very front row of cars that faced the bandstand.

And there was to be special music. Sam Lewellyn had seen to that. Indeed, practically the whole concert was to have a single theme. All the old love songs that Plovers Run bands had ever played were to be revived.

One by one, the members of the band were at last climbing the steps of the stand, wearing their white coats and blue caps. And now Sam himself had appeared. He was wearing a red rose in one of the soft white lapels of his coat. In a few minutes all the horns were pointed toward him. He now stood in a flood of white light with one hand lifted; with the other he balanced the cornet against his lips. There was a long moment of silence, a kind of disappointed, questioning silence, everywhere along the street. Why was Sam beginning the concert before Eliakim and the bride had arrived? As the music began, people slowly came to understand. Sam had planned the first piece as a prelude. It was to serve as a kind of belated wedding march. The music began with a sudden blare, but changed quickly to a gay, jaunty beat. Soon it had softened into a slow, drifting rhythm. The people in the cars and on the sidewalks were recognizing the old melody of "A Bicycle Built for Two." Here and there a voice was rising from the crowd, singing the words of the song. The voices quickly multiplied. Soon they were rising in full chorus everywhere. The band played still more slowly, suiting its pace to the voices. The song rolled and surged all the way along the street now, the words rising in a definite unison.

Daisy, Daisy, give me your promise true,
I'm most crazy, all for the love of you.
We'll not have a stylish marriage,
For we can't afford a carriage,
But you'll look sweet, upon the seat
Of a bicycle built for two.

The song became more and more regular and stately. It rose in great swells that went drifting up toward the soft stars of a quiet summer sky.

But suddenly there was a slight commotion farther back in the street, followed by a few sharp honks from automobile horns; everyone knew Eliakim Brown and the bride were arriving. Ben Parker stepped out into the open lane running the length of the street between the rows of solidly parked cars. With his long marshal's flashlight he began signaling the newcomer to drive forward through the lane. The singing had suddenly stopped, but the band music spurted and grew louder till it soon became a wild, maddening dance of sound.

The two headlights came, at first slowly, along the lane between the cars. Ben Parker kept waving his flashlight expansively, in a cordial welcome. Then, suddenly, the lights seemed to come toward him with wild lurching jumps. A moment later he was barely able to step out of the way. As the car leaped into the wide circle of light falling from the bandstand, everybody saw that it was the new Ford coupe. Eliakim seemed to be gripping the steering wheel as if he would tear it from its fastenings, and Lena, half-risen from her seat, was clinging frantically to Eliakim's shoulders. With several violent jumps the car went across the circle of light just as the band burst into still louder, wilder music. Up in the stand Sam Lewellyn was beating the air high above the blaring and swaying horns. A moment later the Ford lunged madly at the stand. There was a long crashing and splintering. Sam Lewellyn's horn was flying far out into the street in a flashing arc. And then Sam himself was flung violently backward. Through the broken railing he fell sprawling over the shiny top of the car.

Quick shrieks and screams rose everywhere from the parked cars. A moment later the whole street fell into hushed silence. Two men were pulling Sam Lewellyn down from where he lay sprawled over the top of the car. Others were trying to open the jammed door of the coupe. Someone cried sharply for a doctor. Then Doc Beringer came, in his white duck trousers and hatless, running down from the street. In the silence people could hear his heavy puffing as he trotted out through the wide circle of light. They were extricating Mrs. Brown from the car now. For a moment she lay limp in the arms of two of the men. Just as Doc Beringer touched her forehead, she seemed to leap out of the arms of the men. She ran screaming to the other side of the car. Eliakim was already out on the street, and had stepped quickly back from the men who were offering to support him. There was a dark smear of blood on his long narrow brow. Lena flew toward him. Trembling and sobbing, she stood clinging to his neck.

Eliakim, standing at his full height, was staring fixedly down at the car. His face was very stern, and his eyes seemed to be burning out from under the dark smear on his forehead. At last he turned to Sam Lewellyn, who was standing now at some distance supported by two other men. "Sam," Eliakim's voice was very hard and low, and strangely steady. "It was you got me into this. Now you get me home out of it. That's what you do." Sam tried to speak, but couldn't. He was shaking like a leaf.

In just a little while one of the mechanics from the garage had driven a Ford sedan up close to the bandstand. Eliakim looked at it angrily, but finally decided to get into the car. Lena tried to climb through the narrow door almost simultaneously with him, for she seemed unwilling to let go of his arm for an instant. The car moved slowly off along the street. Then the doctor was helping Sam Lewellyn away. Sam walked with a heavy limp out of the circle of white light.

It was nearly two hours later before most of the cars had left town. One by one, they had gone, as if reluctantly. The street was almost empty now. The bandstand stood alone, still flooded with white light and in all its decorations, but with one of its sides smashed in, and beside it was the shiny new Ford coupe with its nose bashed far back into its vitals.

The next morning Mickey Coffins was in town with a team and a wagon. The hired man, who was still staying over at Lena's place, was with him. Mickey's face was suspiciously serious, for there was the slightest hint of a grin upon his lips. When he went down to Sam Lewellyn's house, he found Sam in bed with a big bandage covering the side of his head. Mickey would answer none of Sam's questions. He simply said that he had come to town with instructions from Eliakim to bring the Ford back out to the farm, and to tell Sam Lewellyn that he was to keep his hands strictly off the car. Mickey made his announcement in a solemn voice, but with the grin spreading, as if in spite of himself, over his face. He would stop for no explanations, even though Sam's pleading voice followed him all the way out of the bedroom. He merely stopped at the door, grinned back at Sam, and was gone.

A short while later Mickey and Lena's hired man were puffing the Ford out of the soiled and torn bunting of the bandstand. They dragged the car slowly away behind the wagon. Two dozen aproned storekeepers came to their doors, and several boys followed in the street. At last the Ford went out of sight amidst the thick shade of maples at the end of Main Street.

During the next few days Plovers Run did nothing but talk of the accident. By Saturday Sam Lewellyn was able to get down to the garage again, with a smaller bandage over his right ear. He told the story of the accident scores of times during the day. On Saturday night little groups of farmers were continually examining the bandstand, and standing for long discussions near the spot where the Ford had crashed. Plovers Run, the more it talked about the whole affair, seemed to find it more and more difficult to believe its own tongue.

Then Plovers Run learned that there would be no concert on the coming Wednesday evening. This was Monday. Sam Lewellyn simply didn't feel that he would be equal to it yet. Besides, two of the other musicians had broken fingers. Sam, with the other business men, had decided to call the concert off for this one Wednesday evening. Instead, Sam thought he might go out to Eliakim's place that evening. He was feeling able to do a little driving now. It wouldn't hurt to go out there anyway. Something might be done about repairing the car. He could have a talk with Eliakim anyway. Maybe something might come of it.

As Sam left town, driving toward the South County Road, people saw him and wondered. It was the first time in years that Sam Lewellyn had been out of Plovers Run on a Wednesday evening in summer, and it seemed very strange. Everyone felt almost superstitious about it. There was something ominous about such a thing.

Sam was driving very slowly. There was no hurry about getting out to Eliakim's. Besides, he felt a little dizzy yet, especially from the movement of the car. He wouldn't even stop at Mickey Collins's, for Mickey would talk for an hour or two and he didn't want that. It would be getting early dusk after a little while. He'd just about get out to Eliakim's and have time to take a good look at the coupe by daylight. Eliakim surely wouldn't mind him coming out and looking at the car anyway. Probably be glad about it. Wednesday evening this way, and no concert to go to. Kind of like to have company, maybe. Leastwise they could talk things over.

It was not till Sam had pulled up in front of Eliakim's gate that he noticed anything strange. He was stepping out of the car when his eye first caught the flash of metal out in one of the small lots just beyond the house and barn. Sam could now see that it was the shiny top of the new Ford coupe reflecting the brilliant red sunlight that was bathing everything. Only the top of the car was visible, for the coupe was all but hidden amidst a great pile of brushwood and old fence planks and barrels and boxes. Sam stood for some time, helplessly staring out toward the feedlot. Then he saw Eliakim. The latter had suddenly stepped out from the side kitchen door. For a few moments Eliakim remained motionless. He was hatless, and he seemed preternaturally stiff and tall against the streaming red light. He was gazing defiantly out toward the road, straight at Sam who stood still with one hand resting doubtfully on the low wicket gate. At last Eliakim went back into the house, then shortly returned, carrying a large yellow can. He walked away, taking long resolute strides through the light in the direction of the feedlot. Then Lena had burst out from the kitchen door. She stood watching Eliakim anxiously, her hands clutched into her apron.

A few moments later a great blaze was leaping up from the pile of brushwood and boxes about the coupe. In a little while it had risen to a solid pointed flame. A loud cracking and whirring now came steadily through the still air.

Sam Lewellyn stood at the gate, his whole face drawn into an incredulous stare. His eyeballs seemed to be growing large and dry with staring. Then, after some time, he knew that Eliakim Brown was coming toward him across the lawn. He was bringing Lena with him, leading her by the hand. But there was nothing defiant about him now. His stride seemed almost jaunty. The hard lines of his face were breaking into a queer grin. "Glad to see you, Sam." There was only the slightest hint of sternness in his voice. "Thought you'd be out one of these times. Been just waitin' for you to come. Wanted to show you something. Wanted to show you how I could fix that fancy gig you sold me." Eliakim stopped for a few moments, scrutinizing Sam's face. "I ain't ready to die yet, Sam. Not by a long shot, I ain't. When I get ready to do that I'm goin' to do it decent. I ain't the kind that wants to go around tryin' to kill hisself." There was a short jerky laugh, and Eliakim was silent.

Afterward, Sam was not sure just what he had said to Eliakim. In telling the whole story, all he could do was to place the emphasis upon Lena. During the first few days after the fire, he was constantly explaining how the woman had stood there that evening, listening to all that Eliakim had said with large tears in her eyes. The woman understood what a car would have meant to them. She could appreciate it. But a week later Mickey Collins was denying the possibility of this. He had had his own private reasons for not going too near Eliakim's place too soon after the fire. But three days later he had found Eliakim burying the remains of the Ford in a corner of the feedlot; as he reported it in Plovers Run, he had even found Eliakim whistling while he worked. But as for Lena, he had found her hanging up a washing in the back yard; and never had Mickey seen a man's clothes, and especially a man's underclothes, washed so spotlessly clean. It was incontrovertible proof that Lena's love had suffered no substantial change, and that the incident of the Ford had made no serious difference.

In such a debate it was hard for Plovers Run to decide finally and certainly. Sam Lewellyn's word was more dependable on most matters, on cars, and even on most of the higher things of life, such as music. But Mickey Collins had already been proved a prophet, and he was on the true old side of happy endings. Usually Plovers Run listened to him, and wished earnestly that it could believe.

17.

TOMORROW AFTERNOON

It had been so quiet and comfortable, living there beside the old road. Mrs. Paley was always remembering the way it used to be especially on summer afternoons, with the great wagons full of wheat going along in the deep dust, and sometimes people like the Martins and the Baileys going into Marlton in their carriages, and always waving to her when she was out in the yard.

But mostly she liked to remember the big green house just across the road, where Mrs. Kevins lived. Every summer afternoon Mrs. Paley would go over to visit Mrs. Kevins. She would put on her dark blue dress with the lace fringe around the neck and the lace cuffs, and then she would go down the narrow path and across the dusty road for her visit. She would always find Mrs. Kevins sitting in her great willow chair, out on the cool porch with the big green pillars, back behind all the flowers and the thick vines. She would be sitting with her white hands folded on her dark organdy lap, and her white hair brushed back tight against her thin face. And sometimes, when she was at her needlework, Mrs. Kevins would have her little shiny glasses on. At first Mrs. Paley felt kind of awkward and timid, coming over just to visit this way. But she could tell that Mrs. Kevins always liked for her to come, because when she saw her coming up along the gravel path between the thick beds of four o'clocks, she would always take her glasses off very quickly, and say, "Oh, Mrs. Paley, so you've come. I'm so glad, I've just been waiting for you." And after a while it got so it didn't seem strange at all, coming over every afternoon to visit Mrs. Kevins this way.

And then Mrs. Kevins would always have tea. Maybe one of Mrs. Kevins' granddaughters, who used to stay with her sometimes, would bring out the tea, with the blue and white cups and saucers—Mrs. Kevins' cups were so thin and frail, and there was a silver teapot, a beautiful pot with a thin, curving neck. Mrs. Paley never took but one cup of tea, even when Mrs. Kevins took two cups. And sometimes when Mrs. Kevins was telling her about something very important she almost forgot to drink any of her tea at all. Mrs. Kevins loved to talk and talk about things—about her flowers, her morning-glories and pansies and four-o'clocks, and about her little granddaughters and their pink dresses and the things they were always doing and saying. And sometimes Mrs. Kevins would tell about people down in Marlton. Mrs. Paley thought it was wonderful how she seemed to know everything that was going on. She always knew when people were sick, or got married. And when people died she knew all about their funerals. And when anybody moved away from Marlton she always told Mrs. Paley that it seemed just like everybody was moving away.

Mrs. Paley would sit listening to Mrs. Kevins talking this way until the sun was a great low flame piercing into the shade of the porch through the tangle of vines. Then she would rise and say that she must get over home—she had no idea it was getting so late. As she went slowly down the gravel path she would stop to look for a moment at the four-o'clocks, and again, just before going over the narrow, dusty road, to wave a quick sedate goodbye to Mrs. Kevins. Then all during the evening over at home, while she was getting her supper, and later, when she was sitting at her little window that looked out toward the green house across the road, Mrs. Paley would be thinking of her visit with Mrs. Kevins.

In the evenings, when she would be sitting in her window, it seemed as though she hardly knew anybody in Marlton now except Mrs. Kevins. Ever since Mr. Paley had died from the heat that time he was coming home from the grocery store, she had lived here alone, and all these years Mrs. Kevins had been so nice to her. It even seemed as though she didn't hardly care to know anybody except Mrs. Kevins. It was so wonderful living just across from her big green house this way, and going over every afternoon and drinking tea with her, and talking about everything on the big shady porch back behind the flowers and the vines. . . .

But all that was so very long ago. Mrs. Paley had not really seen Mrs. Kevins for years, not since that strange day when all those men came up the old dusty road with their huge smoking machines, and began building the new pike that ran out of Marlton. The pike which the men built was like a great wall, all yellow and gravelly, and it rose right up from the wicket gate and the low hedge out in front of Mrs. Paley's house. After it was built Mrs. Paley could hardly see Mrs. Kevins' house at all. She couldn't see the porch or the big green pillars, or the flowers or vines, but only the roof and the slender red chimney that ran up into the tops of the quiet maple above the high, level line of the road. Then there were the big green and black motor cars, filled with people in bright yellow hats and scarfs, always flashing past on the great pike. And after that Mrs. Paley could never think of going over to see Mrs. Kevins, for she was afraid of the great cars that kept roaring and whirring past, and the new pike that rose right up in front of her little wicket gate always seemed so terribly high and so steep.

But just at that hour in the afternoon when she used to go over the old road to Mrs. Kevins', she would often go down now to her wicket gate, and stand there timidly gazing over the pike above her, at the sharp, high corners of Mrs. Kevins' roof and the slender chimney rising into the tops of the maple trees. Sometimes she would start quickly forward through the gate, as if to go on over the road. But always the great yellowish slope would rise up so steep and so high above her, and the great cars would come again, rushing and roaring so terribly close, just there above her head. Then she would become bewildered and stand there with one hand pulling nervously at the little fringe of lace about her throat. And suddenly she would shrink back inside the gate again, remaining there as before with her hands gripping the wickets. After that she would continue staring across the road for a long time, until at last she could see wisps of white smoke above the red chimney, disappearing in the blue sky beyond. Now she knew that Mrs. Kevins must be making her tea. She wondered if Mrs. Kevins was out on the porch now, and if the little girls in the pink dresses were bringing out the thin blue and white cups and saucers. And then she would begin to wonder if Mrs. Kevins was waiting for her...but...but Mrs. Kevins would understand, it was getting so late now...and she would have to wait till tomorrow...she would have to wait and go over to Mrs. Kevins' tomorrow afternoon. It would be so nice then, going over to the big cool porch tomorrow afternoon and drinking tea with Mrs. Kevins and talking with her just like she always did...

After that Mrs. Paley's thin old face would suddenly brighten, would seem less pale and timid, and she would be smiling up as if at the flashing cars which she really did not see at all. The people in the cars sometimes noticed the old lady standing behind the low green hedge. Some of them wondered at the lifted, smiling face that seemed so strangely lit. A few smiled in return. Others only turned to smile to their companions. But none of them ever noticed that the old lips were always trembling, as if vainly trying to whisper something—something about Mrs. Kevins and tomorrow afternoon.

When the dusk had come and had deepened almost to darkness, Mrs. Paley would at last turn, and go with jerky, shuffling steps back along the narrow path to her house. After that a small window would suddenly fill with light that seemed to brighten gradually as the night grew darker. Finally the light would go out, and Mrs. Paley's house would be entirely swallowed into the shadows under the road.

Then at last there came a warm summer afternoon when on the other side of the great pike the beds of four-o'clocks were very bright and gay in front of Mrs. Kevins' big green house, and people in the passing cars, turning to look at the flowers, saw at the end of a gravel path a large black wreath upon the door. The people who saw this spoke to their companions in the passing cars only about the flower beds and how pretty they were. Few said anything about the black cloth which they saw upon the door.

That afternoon, as usual, Mrs. Paley was standing out at her own wicket gate, occasionally smiling vaguely as she gazed up at the road. No one in the passing cars noticed her, and she hardly heard the snarling and whining of the racing wheels above her. She seemed merely staring over the road at the tops of the maple trees and the slender red chimney leaning so idly against a high wall of intense blue sky.

But suddenly her hands gripped the sharp tops of the wickets until the white bones of their knuckles seemed bursting through the withered skin. Mrs. Paley could not tell whether it was someone coming over the road and down the steep bank toward her. She was not sure until her eyes had fluttered nervously several times and she looked again as steadily as she could. Then she saw that it was a tall man dressed in very black-looking clothes who was coming right down from the great road to the gate where she was standing. As he came nearer she could see him taking off his hat, and then she could see that his face looked very serious and sad.

He was talking to her now. "Mrs. Paley," he was saying in a deep, strange voice, "Mrs. Paley, I must tell you that... Mrs. Kevins...at nine o'clock this morning. I believe she was a close friend of yours..."

Mrs. Paley was trembling violently now. Her wrinkled chin shook helplessly beneath her sunken mouth that kept twisting and pulling back and forth in her pale face. But she couldn't understand the man's words. Though his voice was very loud and clear, his words seemed strange and very far away. Suddenly the man's loud voice seemed to come very near...

"Mrs. Kevins asked that you be brought to her...no one supposed she would go so soon... If you wish to come over to the house for a little while..."

Then the tall man's words became part of a wild moaning and screaming of wheels upon the road above. Mrs. Paley could not understand the meaning of the words at all, they seemed so strange and so far away. And now they were gone away altogether, swallowed into the moaning and screaming on the road above her. One of her hands was picking at the lace collar of her dress, while the other gripped the sharp tops of the wicket gate. But now she was trying to speak. She would tell the tall man that she couldn't go over to Mrs. Kevins' today...that it was too late, that she would go over to Mrs. Kevins' tomorrow, in the afternoon, before it was too late like this. Yes, she would go over then...and have tea with Mrs. Kevins, and she would talk with Mrs. Kevins...and...

But the tall man was now coming even closer to her, and he was talking to her again. His strange deep voice seemed to be saying something about Mrs. Kevins...it was more queer than ever what the tall man was saying...she couldn't understands at all the words which his deep, loud voice kept saying to her.

Her head was now thrust silently forward, doubtfully. Her small face had grown hard and fixed with pained bewilderment. She heard the tall dark man still talking to her. Then, after a long while, his voice suddenly became faint and blurred, and she could hardly hear him at all. After that he seemed to be going away. She saw him, very dark and very tall, as he went over the steep, high pike. Then he was suddenly gone.

Mrs. Paley kept staring over the road for a long time, her face still thrust forward painfully. Now she could see the slender chimney again, and the steep roof and the tops of the trees above the pike. But the chimney, the roof, the trees were dim to her eyes, as if strange quiet shadows were gathering everywhere about them. Yes, yes, she hurriedly told herself, she must wait now. It was too late. It was too late to go over to Mrs. Kevins' for tea now.

Mrs. Paley turned quickly from the gate and the road and jerked hurriedly up the gravel path to her yellow house, where she stopped in the door and looked back at the high road again. Then she remembered the tall strange man. She tried to think what his deep, sad voice had been saying to her. But she couldn't remember his words at all. They seemed to have gone somewhere...very far away...

Now the flashes of passing light were flickering upon the house hidden beneath the shadows of the great road. After a while the small window was suddenly filled, as usual, with yellow light. As the thinner darkness of the early night deepened steadily the window seemed to brighten until it was like a small eager eye peering out over the high black wall of the road. Then after a long time the light in the window went out, and the strong fierce lights on the road flashed by as before, and wheels screamed for a moment, then were silent. But back in the darkened window an old lady stood for a long time, gazing quietly beyond the road toward where the tops of trees swayed gently and a slender chimney leaned upon the blackness. The old lady scarcely saw the wild flashes of light at all, nor heard the screaming wheels. She was very quiet. She was thinking of tomorrow, and smiling into the darkness.

18.

PUBLIC AUCTION

Lydia sat in one of the two brown-leather chairs that were not yet packed. Over beneath a curtainless window a square of bright winter sunlight lay on the bare floor of the parlor. The air in the big room was chilly and dead.

A child, wrapped in white woolens, was clinging to the woman's knee. Lydia held the child's hands absently in her lap as she gazed out at the floor in front of her. A dark shawl fell down over her heavy blue dress. Her young face was white and strained under her dark piled hair.

At times the white face would be startled to a tenser nervousness by scattered shouting from outside, followed always by men's broken laughter. Once in a while a motor would splutter and moan for a short time, to be quickly swallowed by a rising jabber of voices. The shouting seemed to grow more shrill, the laughter more loud and frequent. The woman's thin lips flinched and trembled in her young face. She sat very stiffly in the chair, her head bent slightly forward.

Suddenly the child slipped from her knee. Lydia's hand reached quickly after it. But the child went tottering on through the square of sunlight. Two pink fists reached up to the window sill. The small yellow head became a ball of silk in the brilliant light.

The woman swept over to the window and bent impulsively over the child. As she rose hesitantly, one hand still rested on the child's shining head. Timid and bewildered, the woman's eyes looked out through the window.

Out beyond the low iron gate of the yard, Lydia saw small groups of men gathered everywhere over the farmlot. They were standing amidst large piles of machinery, harness, and small tools. Along the fence that ran out from the barn, several horses were tied in a row, their rumps glistening in the sun, their tails tied up neatly in bright colored ribbons. Cattle moved in a pen farther away, their red backs alternating dark and shiny in the sun.

Lydia's strained eyes returned to the farmlot. Suddenly they became fixed upon a high pile of household things over in a corner. She saw her big oval dining table and several straight-backed chairs. The sides and springs of a bed leaned against the warming ovens of a range stove. The blue top of a washing machine shone in the light. Slightly to one side of the pile of things, Lydia saw the high white doors of her kitchen cabinet. She was staring out into the farmlot now with wide eyes and a slight jerking at her mouth.

The men were beginning to move about, looking at the horses, examining the plows and harness. They seemed very big and rough in their dirty sheepskin coats and muddy overalls that bagged far out over their high overshoes. Brief shouts were rising above the steady mutter and babble of voices. And now a voice came more shrilly than the others. "Hey, Lute," it was shouting, "you goin' to buy all them pitchforks and shovels? You must be figurin' on goin' to work." A bellow of laughter rose from the whole farmlot. Then Lydia noticed a big man standing directly in front of the kitchen cabinet, his hat pushed far back on his head. He reached up to open the white doors. She heard a high cracked voice calling to him. The words came very clear. "What you want that for, Jake?" the strained voice was shouting. "You can't hide none a your liquor in that." The laughter crashed and rolled in the farmlot for some time. The jabber of voices rose again, slowly.

Lydia's young face remained startled and afraid. Instinctively, she moved slightly back from the window, where she stood, slender and tall, and quite motionless in the streaming sunlight. At her knee, the baby seemed fascinated by all the movement and noise, sometimes breaking into a gay babbling at the window. Occasionally the woman's long lashes would lower over her eyes, as if to shut out the sight of the men in the farmlot. She would be looking steadily down at the child, her high bosom lifting and falling under her dark dress. As her eyes were slowly raised again, they seemed to grow almost hard and blazing. The quick tightness of anger pressed into her small lips.

Suddenly Lydia was gazing at Ben's face. He was coming out of the barn, along with three or four other men. His hat was pushed far back on his head, his big sheepskin thrown out wide from his open throat. He and the others were laughing and talking loudly. Lydia knew instantly what it meant. Yelling and laughing and making a fool of himself again. Treating the men. Having whiskey for them there in the barn. She saw him now, his legs braced apart, standing amidst a group of men who were looking at the horses. He was talking loudly and waving an arm toward the animals. Lydia saw all the men looking at him, listening intently, leaning forward as if to catch his words. But one little man in a dirty leather coat was grinning and edging around in front of him. The little man said something out of his sharp monkey-like face, then turned and went over to the horses, where he stooped cautiously to feel the hind leg of one of the animals. He looked up impudently from the horse's leg, grinning and shaking his head knowingly. There was a burst of laughter. Then the woman saw all the men looking expectantly at Ben. After a few moments he strode over to the little man, grasped him by the coat collar and pulled him away from the horse. He was leading the little man toward the barn now. The crowd again broke into a prolonged roar of laughter. After some time the two returned from the barn, the little man almost in a trot as he was led directly back to the horse. Lydia saw that the little man was grinning now, almost sheepishly. She noticed Ben's face, grinning and flashing toward the crowd. The little man stooped once more, and felt the horse's leg. This time he did not shake his head, but rather turned his small face up to all the men with a kind of surprised and incredulous smile. There was another burst of laughter, louder than before. Lydia saw Ben standing beside the horse, his hand resting on the animal's buttock, one of his legs thrown jauntily over the other, his hat tossed still farther back upon his gleaming black hair. His face was pulled half sidewise in an easy, confident smile. The laughter became wild and riotous as the little man stepped back among the crowd. Lydia shrank slightly back from the window. Her hand had pulled the child's head closely into her dress.

The crowd of men were now moving over to a hay ladder that stood in the middle of the farmlot. A long-legged man was clambering onto the wagon. He was dressed differently from the others. He wore a black derby hat that looked blueish gray in the bright sunshine. His light tan coat was long and fastened about the middle with a belt. A bright red tie was bundled into a big knot just beneath his sharp, long chin. The man was suddenly grinning confidently down at the crowd and holding a shiny cane out over their upturned faces as if commanding silence.

The man stepped gingerly over to the edge of the wagon. He handed his cane and hat graciously down to one of the men. After unbuckling his coat, and removing it dexterously in a single movement of his long body and arms, he laid it on the wagon at his feet, then reached once more for his hat and cane. Stepping back to the middle of the wagon, he swept his hat grandly onto his reddish hair. With his cane he flipped the ends of the brilliant tie from under the lapels of his tight gray body coat. The tie fluttered impishly out from his long chin. The cane swept over the crowd again, this time with a long swaggering flourish. The jabber and laughter of the men dropped abruptly into silence.

"Gentlemen," the man shouted, as if demanding still closer attention from the circle of faces beneath him, "I have the privilege of standing before you in the name of Ben Thorn." The shrill ringing voice stopped for a moment. "Gentlemen, it's an honor—Ben Thorn."

A quick shout rose from the men. The woman saw her husband leap onto the hay ladder with one swing of his great shoulders. He was sweeping his big felt hat to his knees and bowing. As he rose to his full height he turned to the tall man in the faded derby. "Let her go," he shouted, laughing, "Go to it, Jim." Then he whirled and leaped wildly out amidst the crowd. Lydia saw his doubled knees and big overshoes narrowly miss several hats near the wagon. There was a quick rift in the crowd where Ben was jumping. Then a shaking and swaying of shoulders went all around the hay ladder. Another short burst of laughter came from the farmlot.

The man in the blueish derby had stepped over to the edge of the wagon again. The crowd was once more silent as the cane flashed out over the upturned faces. Lydia saw Ben standing among the men, his face lifted in a grinning challenge to the auctioneer. "Gentlemen," the man was crying in a voice that rose immediately to a steady whanging chant. "Today you have the chance of your lives. One of the greatest sales ever held in Fountain County. Ben Thorn says sell, no matter what she brings. It's a clean sweep, boys, and the low man buys. Not a by-bidder on the grounds. Ben Thorn is a sellin' out. And you boys know Ben Thorn. When he says sell out, he don't mean back out. The low man buys, gentlemen. Yes, sir, and we got anything and everything you want. It's the chance of a granddad's lifetime. Don't go home without buyin', boys. Don't disappoint the women folks."

The shrill voice suddenly dropped to a steadier, more matter-of-fact tone, but still came in a level chant. "You boys know the terms. It's twelve months, approved notes, and seven per cent interest. And remember, five per cent for cash." Then the voice rose, as shrill and rapid as before. "So here goes, boys, your money talks. And it can't talk wrong at Ben Thorn's sale."

As the high voice went on, the man's jaws and mouth and brows seemed to work on hinges. The blueish derby bobbed and swayed mechanically. The cane kept flashing, and always the bright tie danced beneath the man's long smooth chin. Suddenly the cane came down stiffly. The man was pointing over at a corner of the farmlot.

There was a few moments' lull in the high chant. Two men were going over to the farmlot fence. Then Lydia saw them returning with the blue washing machine. Her eyes were instantly wide and desperate. Her mouth fell loosely open in her white face. The whanging chant came again, more sharp and rapid than before.

"And here we' are, boys. This brand new washer. Good as new. Step right up, boys, see for yourselves. Startin' off right with this washer. And I tell you why. Some of you fellers look like you need it worse than anything we got at this sale."

There was a great snort of laughter. Some of the men pointed across the hay ladder at friends. "That's for you, Mart," a deep voice shouted from the crowd, "he's a talkin' to you." The laughter continued until the auctioneer's cane had again commanded silence.

"And what do I hear, boys? What do I hear for this brand new washing machine? Don't be backward about saying you need it. We know it anyway." Another short laugh was choked off abruptly, lest any of the auctioneer's words should be missed.

"What do I hear there? That's it. Seth Howard, four dollars and a half, and Seth Howard starts it. Seth, you don't need it half as much as some of these fellers." The chant was slowed and broken for a moment as the auctioneer looked down into a big face grinning up foolishly from the crowd. "But who says five? Five, and who wants it? Four and a half and going five. Gib Purvis. Gib says five and looks like he wants it. Five and a half now, five and a half. A brand new washing machine. Who says five and a half?"

Lydia was now looking out into the farmlot with a helpless, fascinated gaze. The cane still danced and flashed above the heads, and the derby swayed and bobbed perpetually. Suddenly the auctioneer's cane dropped before one of the men. Lydia could tell it was the little man, who was standing very close to the edge of the wagon. The cane was lifted quickly, flipping up the little man's wide hat. "Look up here, Nate," the auctioneer shouted with mock gruffness. "You ought to be listening to this mighty particular. Aren't you going to buy this washing machine? You need it, Nate, and no use denying it. You're the feller to take this washing machine home."

The little man's face had grown very red. He looked up at the auctioneer, and then at some of the men standing about him. There was a bewildered, helpless grin on his face. At last he nodded his head hesitantly.

"That's the stuff," the auctioneer cried, looking out over the crowd. "Nate Sims says he wants this washing machine for five and a half, and he's going to be wearing a clean undershirt Saturday night. And now who says six? Five and a half, and who'll make it six?"

The voice went on, and the man kept moving from side to side of the wagon. He had pushed the derby far back on his head now, and his cane was sweeping and dancing and pointing over the crowd. The woman still heard the occasional bursts of laughter. But the voice of the auctioneer was slowly becoming a kind of beating pain in her mind, something fierce and sharp that kept rising out there in the still sunlight, and then, in the aching emptiness within her.

Finally her eyes were flicked open in a fixed gaze. Two men were lifting the bed onto the wagon. The auctioneer was now holding one of the gleaming white bed posts and his cane was pointed out confidently over the wide circle of faces. Lydia's gaze again found Ben's tall shoulders and lifted face. He was still standing with his hands thrust down into his overalls, looking up at the auctioneer with an amused grin. Once more she heard scraps of the twanging chant...

"Just what you been lookin' for, boys...here's a chance for you fellers to find out what a real sleep means...you fellers that were born that way especially... And it's as strong as they make 'em... Just look at those springs, and that mattress...the mattress goes with the bed, boys... And it'll hold anybody.... Yes, sir, and his wife too, no matter what she weighs...and..." The auctioneer's cane dropped back over his shoulder as he cupped his hand to his mouth. The woman did not hear his words now, but the men broke into thunderous laughter. One snorting guffaw followed another. The men swayed and rocked, and with a wagging of heads looked closely into each other's faces.

A deep crimson had shot into Lydia's face. Her small mouth grew tight and hard. Her eyes blazed between the narrowing lids. She saw the men still swaying, still heard the roaring of their laughter. As her eyes opened slightly, she saw Ben standing motionless in the crowd. He didn't seem to be swaying and laughing with the other men. His face had not changed from its amused grin. Her small mouth was suddenly trembling. For a moment she felt almost grateful to him.

Then the shrill chant went on again, broken frequently by quick cackles of laughter and brief shouts from the crowd. Finally Lydia saw the bed being removed from the wagon. They were lifting something else up to the auctioneer, but she could not tell what it was. Her eyes had become weak and blurred. A sickness was drifting down through her body and limbs. She swayed back from the window, pulling the child with her toward the chair. She slouched slowly down, and leaned forward limply. Her dull eyes were lowered to the small bright head that lay across her knees. After a little the child began to sing and croon in a broken, contented way. At last scraps of the shrill chant came again from the farmlot. Once in a while a bellow of laughter would burst into the house, to go crashing through all the empty rooms. Then the chant would go on again, above the shouts and cries of the men. Once Lydia knew it was Ben's voice. There was a louder snort of laughter. Then he shouted again. The laughter rolled more deeply and wildly than before.

The woman continued to sit motionless in the chair, one of her hands loosely supporting the child's shoulder. The contented babbling still came from her lap. Her head had lifted now, till she was gazing out at the bare boards of the floor. She began speaking, as if to herself. Her voice was low and hard. "Out there like that...making fools of us...making fools of both of us." Her voice died into the stillness of the room. When she spoke again, the words were like tense spitting sounds. "Laughing and yelling with all those men. Buying whiskey for them... Out there, selling his own things...making fools of us.... He doesn't care...yelling and shouting out there, like that.... He...he doesn't care for anything."

The woman pulled the child up into her arms now, hugging it almost fiercely to her breast as she swayed slightly back and forth in the chair. At last she rose slowly, then suddenly went away toward the rear of the house. Her heels clattered loudly as she walked through the undraped double door and across the empty dining room. Just inside the door of the kitchen she stopped before a small white cradle. Stooping, she laid the child gently down, pulling the white woolen blankets carefully about the bright silken head. A fat pink hand reached out through the rungs of the cradle as the woman turned and walked slowly across to a low table.

Lydia was gazing absently down at a pile of pans on the table. Suddenly and angrily she began packing the pans into a large pine box that stood open beside her. A hard banging and clattering filled the silence of the room. Gradually her arms moved more slowly and mechanically at the pans. At last her hands were resting limply on the table, as her young face lifted to the white coldness of the tiled wall before her. Her eyes wandered over to the little curtainless window. Then her gaze went out, beyond high wire fences and a gray orchard, to where green squares of winter wheat lay across the bare sunlit prairie.

She began speaking again, very slowly. "It was this way ever since we came here...just like this...ever since his father died...just crazy all the time...laughing and shouting around the place...these men always coming here, bringing whiskey for him...spending money every way...new cars, and tractors...even the barn.... And you couldn't say a thing...only laugh at you, and go off again that way...not caring at all...just making fools of us...all the time." Lydia's voice had grown quick and thin. Her words dropped bitterly back into the house.

After a short silence, the voice came again, dead and choking. "And now...everything gone...the bank taking everything like that... and him renting now...away out there at Miltonville...everything... everything gone like this. And...and..." The voice became suddenly wild and frantic. "And him out there laughing...laughing and drinking whiskey...and selling everything to all those men..."

The woman's shrill voice went, almost screaming, back through all the empty rooms behind her. Her flushed face jerked violently for a time, then gradually became quiet again. At last her small lips turned sidewise in a bitter smile. There was only a trembling and fluttering of her long lashes as she turned to look out the bare window again. Her gaze became fixed, as before, on the green squares of winter wheat.

There was a sudden knocking somewhere at the front of the house. Lydia's face turned from the small window, her eyes wide and timid as she stared through the dining room. After a few moments she started across the kitchen. As she went on through the other rooms she was smoothing her hair with a nervous hand. In the parlor she stopped to brush her face and eyes with a white wad of handkerchief. Her glance went distractedly over to the window. She saw the tall man in the derby, and the cane still flashing above the wide circle of upturned faces. She heard the shrill voice going on and on. Her eyes suddenly fell upon Ben. For a moment he seemed to be grinning insolently and directly in at her. Her face pulling with pain and doubt, she shrank back toward the middle of the room.

The loud knocking was at the front door again. Lydia turned, and went hesitantly toward the door. Through the long oval glass she could see a shiny car out beyond the brick porch pillars, and the end of the straight front walk. She opened the door slowly. The figures, bundled in heavy clothes, stood against the outer light, slightly to one side in the big porch. The two faces were gazing stolidly in at her. It was Mr. and Mrs. Mann. Lydia saw Cora Mann's old face, long and sharp, with the dead smile drooping down from her eyes and mouth. The old man stood humped and tall, his wide hat bobbing a slow salute out of the background of dead porch vines behind him. He kept grinning foolishly out of his hooked narrow face. Lydia felt the cold eyes and the long straight smile of the woman. Mrs. Mann seemed to be peering directly through her into the empty rooms of the house.

"Is there anything we can do?" the old woman was asking in a cracked singing voice. "We just thought we'd come over. I thought maybe you'd want company whilst the men were all out at the sale."

The old man was bowing stiffly again. Lydia saw his humped shoulders bouncing and jerking down the steps. The two women were stepping into the house. As Mrs. Mann went through the door, her head lifted till her small black hat was perched on her grizzled fur collar. Lydia saw her old eyes grow keen and bright in a quick gaze around the bare room.

Mrs. Mann had edged over toward the window as the door was being closed behind her. Her eyes blinked intently out into the strong sunlight. Her cracked singing voice became soft and familiar now. "Why they's such a big crowd," she was saying. "Ain't they?" As Mrs. Mann turned slyly around, Lydia felt the quick sharp eyes picking and tearing her apart.

The two women moved slowly back from the window. They sat down, stiffly facing each other. As Mrs. Mann's thick, dumpy shoulders leaned out slightly from the back of her chair, her eyes went flitting about the room. "You even got the pictures down, haven't you?" she was saying with eager curiosity. "My how queer it seems without all your nice pictures." There was a silence as Mrs. Mann's squinting gaze went around the walls again. "I remember just how you had them," she went on with a kind of pride. "You had your folks there above the mantle, didn't you? And his'n too. Your husband's was there too, I remember. And his father's was such a good picture. I remember him so well. He was such a fine man, Mr. Thorn was. So steady and dependable like."

Lydia was looking off toward the door of the dining room, her face as gray and hard as steel. Her hands were clasped and pushed deeply into the lap of her dress. At last her eyes flitted back toward Mrs. Mann and her gray lips moved into an expressionless smile.

"And over there on the other wall you had Sir Galyhad, didn't you Lydia? I remember just as well. It was Sir Galyhad, wasn't it? You told me all about the picture once. It was so beautiful, and so noble. And you know what I said. I said it was just like your Ben, Lydia. Just like him." Mrs. Mann's voice had become slow and emphatic. "And it was, wasn't it? So noble and so good, you know."

The old woman's eyes seemed as cold and motionless as two glazed marbles. After a moment or two the voice ran on again, rising quickly till it had a kind of rapid, jangling cadence. "And then I remember the meadow picture. You had it back here, didn't you? I can just see it there yet, so nice and bright above your blue sofa. What are you doing with your blue sofa, Lydia? Are you taking it with you? I just know you wouldn't give that up."

Lydia had risen quickly from her chair. "I must go and see about Phyllis," she said. The words came, thin and weak from her tight lips. She moved rapidly away through the dining room. A moment later her dark head was bent far over the white cradle beyond the frame of the kitchen door.

The house was silent for a little while. Then Mrs. Mann rose laboriously from her chair and went swaying and tottering toward the kitchen. As she crossed the dining room her eyes darted searchingly into every corner. A moment later her broad shoulders, still bundled in the dark coat with the scraggy fur collar, suddenly filled the door leading into the kitchen.

"Oh, here's your little un," the old woman cried in a quick, trembling screech.

Lydia was still bent close over the cradle. The pink face of the child smiled up contentedly, her little eyes very wide; and bright.

Mrs. Mann was speaking again, almost plaintively. "Can't I help some way?" she asked. "Ain't there something I can do out here?"

Lydia had risen from the cradle. The tip of a white tooth was biting her gray under-lip. "Here," she said at last, turning angrily and pulling a low box from under the sink in the corner of the room, "sit on this then." The old woman settled slowly onto the box as Lydia bent around to the table where the pile of pans still lay. Mrs. Mann watched her slyly. A steady clank and clatter of pans came up from the table.

Finally the older woman started to speak slowly, as if measuring the words carefully. "I was just kind of wondering," she began, fitting the words in between the clanks of the pans, and in a tone that became immediately low and intimate. "I was just wondering about Benjamin. Your husband, you know." Her voice became ridiculously slow and cautious. "I just kind of wondered what you thought, Lydia. Your families and us was always so close, you know. And I just wondered. . . ."

Lydia stood motionless for a few moments, then whirled fiercely around. Her fists were clenched against the sides of her blue apron. Her slender figure was as taut and lithe as a cat's. "What do you mean?" The voice came hot and spurting. "Mrs. Mann, I want to know what you mean." Lydia's eyes were two glinting beads in her hard, blank face.

A slow smile drew up the flabby lines in the older woman's cheeks. "Why," she said, with a kind of jerking sob, "I didn't mean nothing. I didn't mean nothing at all, Lydia." Mrs. Mann's wide eyes blinked uneasily. Lydia was still bent intently over her.

"I guess I better go on in to the other room and sit down now," Mrs. Mann said, very meekly. "Maybe I been bothering you at your work out here."

"Yes, you can go in there." Lydia's eyes flashed over toward the doorway.

The older woman rose heavily from the box. Her face was livid. Her eyes were suddenly hard and angry. Her shoes slapped quickly across the floor and on through the dining room. Lydia saw her hobble slowly past the chair in the parlor. She knew she was in there at the window now. She would be standing in there, looking out at the farmlot and grinning.

The whang and beat of the chant came clearly again, dropping into all the empty rooms. Lydia had leaned back against the table, grasping its edge with a white hand. She could hear the chant more and more plainly now. It was becoming strangely loud and shrill. Then it seemed to have stopped abruptly. A great jabber of voices was slowly rising. Lydia moved quickly to the outer kitchen door. Through the small high glass she saw the men over near the cattle pens and the horses. They were moving back into the farmlot now. The crowd seemed to be breaking up. Lydia's eyes found Ben's high hat and shoulders. He was clapping the auctioneer on the back. Then he shouted something to the crowd. All the men turned toward him. Everywhere the red faces were tossed upward in a long burst of laughter.

Ben was striding off from among the men now. Lydia saw suddenly that he was coming toward the house. Several of the men were following him. They were all laughing and jabbering, and Ben was waving his hand and turning to talk loudly to one after another of them. She realized that they were coming directly up to the kitchen door.

Lydia swept over to the cradle. Snatching the child into her arms, she hurried excitedly away through the dining room. In the parlor she sat stiffly down in one of the chairs, wrapping the child closely into her bosom. Her twitching eyes went out painfully to the opposite wall. She seemed hardly aware of the older woman standing over at the window.

The kitchen door was banged open. There was a shuffling of feet, and the sounds of deep voices came rumbling through the house. And now Lydia felt the figure of Mrs. Mann just above her. The old woman was gazing eagerly out toward the kitchen.

There was a brief clattering of pans at the rear of the house. Lydia's head turned nervously. She saw several men standing about the table in the kitchen. A pile of papers lay before them. One of the men was sitting on the low box. His wide shoulders were bent over the table, where he seemed to be writing laboriously. Occasionally Ben's voice came booming out from among the others. Lydia could not see him within the frame of the kitchen door.

"It's old Mr. Talbot," Mrs. Mann was saying. Her voice was tense and subdued. "It's old Jake Talbot, that's who it is. It's him signin'. Wonder what it was he bought. Just like the Talbot's. Buyin' things cheap at sales."

Lydia heard Mrs. Mann's voice running eagerly on. "Why, there's Gib Purvis. He's been buyin' something. Gettin' something for Sadie maybe. He's awful good to her that way. Wonder why Sadie didn't come. Sadie could of come just as well as not. Why didn't he bring Sadie along if he was comin' to the sale?" The old woman was bending down over the chair. "It would of been nice for you, Lydia, if Mrs. Purvis had come. She's always such good help."

Lydia's face was still strained anxiously toward the kitchen. Suddenly Ben was within the frame of the kitchen door. Lydia saw his head and shoulders sprawled down over the table, his chin cupped in his big hand. He was looking up at the men, grinning and winking to them. A small man in a tight leather coat was writing at the table, bent far down, over the paper. Ben suddenly reached over and pushed the little man's hat far back on his head. "Hey, Nate," Ben shouted almost in the little man's ear, "better take your coat off. You're gettin' hot, workin' like that." A long dinning laughter filled the house. The shoulders of all the men kept shaking violently. Some of them were jabbing others in the ribs. And now two of them actually began pulling the coat from the little man's shoulders. There was a brief struggle, after which the little man stood coatless in the middle of the floor. He joined timidly in the laughter, then sat down at the table again. As he bent over his writing, his blue suspenders became tight over his shoulders. Lydia could see the side of his brow and his sharp straining jaw. She could see Ben still sprawled over the table, grinning and winking up at the other men who kept chuckling and shaking their shoulders. At last the little man was rising from the table. There was a sickly grin on his small square face as he stepped back among the men.

"Oh, there's Newt," Mrs. Mann said excitedly. She had moved slightly toward the dining room. "He's signin'. It's him. He's gone and bought something." Lydia's lowered eyes saw the woman's wide skirts jounce away toward the dining room. A moment later she was standing in the kitchen door, her thick bundled form hiding the table completely.

Ben's deep voice was suddenly filling the house. "Well, look who's here." He was almost shouting it. "If it ain't Gramma Mann. Where'd you come from, anyway? You'd ought to be out there at the sale, takin' care of your old man. He don't know how to act at sales any more. Went and bought one of my windy horses. Where you been anyway, Gramma?"

Lydia's face was bent over the child in her arms, peering toward the kitchen. She saw Mrs. Mann standing in the doorway, her small black hat swaying back and forth. A moment later Ben's red face appeared above the black hair. He was shaking her gently and laughing. Then he turned abruptly and pulled her into the kitchen. "Look what your old man's been doin'," he said in the same deep voice. "Signin' all his money away for windy horses." Mrs. Mann peeped down at the table with a coquettish tilt of her head. Suddenly she bounced over beside her husband who was now sitting, half sidewise, on the low box. She gave a quick, playful pull at one of the old man's ears, and then, with a high foolish squealing, came scampering awkwardly through the dining room.

Lydia saw Mrs. Mann come scurrying into the parlor. She stopped in the middle of the room, turned quickly, and stood grinning back at the men in the kitchen. Her hands were clasped tensely before her deep, low bosom. Her whole body was shaking with excitement. A prolonged chuckling arose in the kitchen.

Suddenly Lydia heard Ben's voice coming through the dining room. He was leading the old man toward the parlor in long bouncing strides, and calling out, "Newt"—shouting it almost in the old man's ear—"let's go in and meet the ladies."

The two were standing there in the middle of the room now, the older man humped, withered, and tall, with his hooked face breaking into a long foolish grin. A mock seriousness had settled into Ben's mouth. Suddenly he stepped over to where Lydia sat with her eyes lowered and fluttering over the child. He bent down toward her and pushed a thick red finger playfully against her nose. Lydia felt his hard cool finger. It was like ice against her hot skin. Then, as he leaned farther over her, she smelt the stink of whiskey on his breath. Her white face snapped up into his. As he stepped back to where the old man was standing, he was grinning down at her again.

The old man began a nervous, embarrassed mumbling. His stiff legs were shuffling backward toward the front door. The old woman was following him now, her face turned in a radiant spreading grin.

"Where you folks going?" The words were a loud complaining cry. "Your barn burnin' down or something?" Ben moved over toward the old man. But Newt was still mumbling and grinning out of his long sharp face. His thin shaky voice seemed to be saying something about chores. He kept bowing himself nearer the door.

Through the wide front doorway Lydia could see Mr. and Mrs. Mann leaving the porch. They were moving down into the pale yellow light of late afternoon. Then Mrs. Mann's face was suddenly back at the door again. "Goodbye," she called into the bare room. "Goodbye, Liddie. I'll see you again before you're gone. I'll come over again." The voice rattled back through the house and the woman was gone. Then Ben was standing there in the door, half sidewise, waving heartily out over the porch steps. His body seemed very tall and lithe as he leaned toward the paling light.

He turned slowly. For a few moments he stood looking down at the woman and child over in the chair. He was coming directly across the room now. "Hi there, old woman," he was saying with a kind of mock gruffness, "why don't you come on out and meet everybody? They're not goin' to run away with you. No, sir, not while I'm around." His hand reached out and cuffed the woman's dark hair almost roughly. As he moved away toward the kitchen, Lydia's eyes were lifted quickly. They were eagerly, intently following him. She saw his smooth hips swing and weave with the movement of his wide shoulders as he went directly across the dining room.

A jabber of voices came from the kitchen again. Then after a little while, the voices seemed to be dropping away. Lydia could see the men now, leaving the kitchen door one after another. They were shaking Ben's hand in slow silences. Only Ben's voice went on, filled at times with a strange, jerky laughter. Then he was talking with the auctioneer, who had been leaning back against the kitchen wall, saying very little, but always shaking his cane when he talked. There were only a few words about the sale. Ben gave the other man a small piece of paper. Then they went out through the kitchen door. An immediate intense stillness seemed to fill all the rooms of the house.

A grayness was dimming the walls of the parlor. The light in the room had grown duller. Lydia slowly rose from the chair, still holding the child in her arms. She went hesitantly over toward the window. A big red car stood out beyond the low iron gate of the yard fence. She saw the small round hat and yellowish coat of the auctioneer as he climbed into the front seat. And now Ben was shoving the little man in beside the auctioneer, and shouting above the quick beat and moan of the motor. He seemed to be saying something about giving rides to people who didn't deserve them. The car moved slowly from the gate and past the tall maples along the fence. The little man's blurred grinning face peered out through the glass door. Then the face was gone. The hum of the motor became gradually fainter, then was silent.

Lydia saw Ben striding slowly away toward the barn, past the hay ladder that stood, bare and angular now, in the middle of the farmlot. The two hired hands came out from the barn. Ben stopped to talk with them for a minute or two. Then the men began carrying the things from the farmlot into the wide driveway of the barn. Lydia knew vaguely that all the things would be stored there for a day or two, till the neighbors would come after them. After a little while she saw the men carrying the kitchen cabinet away. The high white doors swayed crazily above the spread backs of the men. She saw the cabinet go dipping and tottering into the big square of the driveway.

As the men went on working about the barn, a grayish dusk began to creep over the farmlot. It seemed to gather thickly out above the cattle pens, and then about the barn itself. Finally it was smudging out the whiteness of the big building. An early darkness was settling quickly over everything. The dull yellow blurs of two swinging lanterns began moving back and forth in the farmlot. Lydia continued to stand at the darkened window, holding the child in her arms. Her eyes had grown wide, and at times they were two watery beads in the darkness.

At last she turned slowly from the window. As she found her way through the empty rooms, the clack of her heels, even the swish of her skirts seemed loud in the silent house. She felt the soft warmth of the child asleep at her breast as she crossed the dining room, heard its slow quiet breathing just below her face.

She had switched on the electric light in the kitchen, and was now laying the child gently among the blankets in the cradle. With eyes puckered against the dazzling light, she rose from the cradle and went slowly across the room. Almost automatically, she stooped to light the small coal oil stove that had not yet been packed. As she rose, half turning from the stove, a nervous hand brushed her dark hair, and her fluttering eyes moved, as if bewildered, around the glinting tile walls of the kitchen. Thin lines, as of pain, were deepening into her drawn face.

At last she went impatiently back to the stove. There were a hard clanging of pans, then the clatter of a coffeepot, and a little while later, the sharp sounds of eggs being cracked, one after another into a skillet. A popping and spluttering came from the stove and the smell of frying began to spread, warm and heavy, through the room.

A quick rattle came at the door knob. Then Ben stepped into the kitchen, swinging the door slowly closed behind him. With an easy sweep of his arm, he removed his wide hat. He looked around with squinted eyes and a half puzzled smile. After a moment or two he discovered the slender figure of the woman standing motionless beside the stove. He stepped silently over behind her, his chin almost touching her dark piled hair. He was grinning quietly down over her shoulder. Lydia's body became stiff and taut as she continued to gaze down into the bubbling skillet. Her shoulders moved slightly with a quick, violent breathing. She could smell the freshness and coolness of his clothes. She could feel his chin as it seemed to brush lightly against her hair. Then her white face suddenly whirled round from the stove. Her eyes were two narrow glints as she looked fiercely up at the man, "Get away from me," she said in a dry, strangled voice. A row of white teeth shone through her gray lips. "Get away from me," she repeated, "You don't care...you...you..." Her voice broke. Her face jerked convulsively. Her whole body shook as in a spasm. Then she was speaking again, her voice choking and crying. "You don't care... out there making fools of us...yelling...and laughing...selling everything...you...you don't care for anything..." Her voice had become a helpless screaming. She hesitated a moment, then turned back to the stove as if to hide her face from him.

The man stepped quietly back to the middle of the room. With his head dropped slightly before him, he stood smiling gently over at the rigid, slender figure of the woman.

At last there was a whimpering in another corner of the room. The big man turned slowly. A broader grin spread quickly out from his mouth and eyes. He moved across the room, and his dark head was now bent low over the child. A moment later a bubble of laughter came from the cradle.

The woman's face had turned instantly from the stove.

She saw small pink fingers reaching up toward a strand of black hair that fell down from the man's shaded head. Then a big hand was reaching into the cradle. The woman was leaning out from the stove, her face startled and fearful. But the man was rising from the cradle now. He stood almost at his full height, grinning radiantly down at the child. Then he turned away to the black doorway, and with a low chuckling strode off into the darkness of the dining room.

A moment later the woman shrank back from the shadowy doorway. The man's voice was shouting to her out of the blackness of the farther room, "Hey, old woman," he was saying, "when you goin' to have supper ready, anyway? I'm just about starved, I tell you." The vibrant voice came waving and rolling through the house. Then the light in the front room was suddenly snapped on.

The woman saw the man's shining hair and broad shoulders moving across the other room. He sprawled suddenly down into one of the chairs. One long leg was thrown out, stretching far over the floor, and a big knee was hooked limply over an arm of the chair. The light flooded his dark head, seeming to touch the muscles in his open-shirted neck to thick bronze cables. His eyes were closing lightly. In a little while he seemed to be resting in an easy sleep.

Lydia moved out to the middle of the kitchen. She kept watching the man timidly, almost reverently. Slowly an eager, half fearful smile came into her eyes. Finally she turned, as if forcing herself, and went over to the stove. As she continued with the work about the kitchen, she kept stopping to peer into the farther room. Once or twice a quick anger came into her face. Then the smile would be again fluttering across the heavy lashes of her eyes.

CLUNY MEDIA

Designed by Fiona Cecile Clarke, the Cluny Media *logo depicts a monk at work in the scriptorium, with a cat sitting at his feet.*

The monk represents our mission to emulate the invaluable contributions of the monks of Cluny in preserving the libraries of the West, our strivings to know and love the truth.

The cat at the monk's feet is Pangur Bán, from the eponymous Irish poem of the 9th century. The anonymous poet compares his scholarly pursuit of truth with the cat's happy hunting of mice. The depiction of Pangur Bán is an homage to the work of the monks of Irish monasteries and a sign of the joy we at Cluny take in our trade.

"Messe ocus Pangur Bán,
cechtar nathar fria saindan:
bíth a menmasam fri seilgg,
mu memna céin im saincheirdd."

Made in the USA
Middletown, DE
21 July 2021

44235025R00119